MW01128077

J. N. Chaney
Copyrighted Material

www.jnchaney.com

1st Edition

BOOKS BY J.N. CHANEY

The Variant Saga:

The Amber Project

Transient Echoes

Hope Everlasting

The Vernal Memory

Renegade Star Series:

Renegade Star

Renegade Atlas

Renegade Moon

Renegade Lost

Renegade Fleet

Renegade Earth

Renegade Dawn

Renegade Children

Standalone Books:

Their Solitary Way

The Other Side of Nowhere

STAY UP TO DATE

Chaney posts updates, official art, previews, and other awesome stuff on his website. You can also follow him on Instagram, Facebook, and Twitter.

Search for **JN Chaney's Renegade Readers** on Facebook to join the group where readers can come together and share their lives and interests, especially regarding Chaney's books.

For updates about new releases, as well as exclusive promotions, sign up for the VIP mailing list. Head there now to receive a free copy of *The Other Side of Nowhere*.

https://www.subscribepage.com/organic

Enjoying the series? Help others discover the Variant Saga by leaving a review on Amazon.

RENEGADE MOON

BOOK 3 IN THE RENEGADE STAR SERIES

J.N. CHANEY

CONTENTS

For Dustin,
Thank you for all
the late-night gaming sessions.

1

"YOU SURE YOU CAN HANDLE THIS?" I asked, holding a training stick in the middle of a large room.

Abigail gave me a strange look, like I must be crazy to think I could beat her in one-on-one combat. "I invited you down here," she said, spinning the staff in her hand. "If you'll remember."

"I was just being polite, in case you wanted an out," I said.

"Me? What about you?"

"Don't worry about me, Sister," I said with a slight smirk.

She cocked her brow. "You know I'm not a nun anymore, don't you?"

"Once a nun, always a nun," I said as she raised her

staff, and a small spark lit up on the other end. We were using electrified weapons in order to test the strength of the shield. It was a safer, albeit still dangerous, alternative to actual gunfire.

Abigail bent her knees and took her fighting stance, giving me a slight nod.

I grinned. "Okay, then," I said, tapping the switch on my own staff. Sparks emitted from the ends.

I immediately rushed forward, swinging the stick in a low sweep as I went for her legs.

She blocked it, pushing the staff aside with her own, then twisted around and managed to strike my shoulder.

"Shield at 98 percent," said the voice in my ear. It was Athena's, the Cognitive program in charge of *Titan*, our present location.

"Damn," I muttered, noticing the blue flicker of the shield as it appeared over my body.

"Looks like the shield works," said Abigail, stepping toward me again, extending the stick towards my chest.

I deflected it, but only barely avoiding the electric sparks as they came within centimeters of my shield. With Abigail off balance, I went for another strike.

She dodged out of the way, but I wouldn't give her time to come back. I swept low again, knowing she'd block it, holding her staff up with mine as she held it across her chest horizontally.

Then I pushed my stick forward, sliding it beneath her staff, and tapped her directly in the chest.

Sparks collided with the shield as a soft blue layer appeared around her. "Dammit," she snapped. "96 percent remaining."

"Two percent more than your hit," I said, winking. "Must be my man-strength."

"You're an idiot," she said, giving me a look.

I ignored her obvious jealousy. "Makes me wonder how many bullets this thing can take."

She nodded. "Should we continue until the shields drain? We can test ammunition later, if you'd like."

I responded with a thrust, stabbing at her face with the stick. She blocked it, then tapped me in the leg for a quick hit.

"Shield at 96 percent," I heard Athena say.

I pushed her stick away, going for a middle thrust, but she deflected.

She pressed forward on her leg, signaling her next move, so I got ready for it. When she lunged, I brushed her staff aside and grabbed hold of her arm, spinning her around so she fell across my leg.

She caught my wrist with her hand, yanking me to the floor with her, and I let go of the stick in the confusion. She managed to get on my waist, holding her stick above my neck, about to press down. I grabbed it, pushing the end. It lowered a few centimeters, causing the shield to flicker as the wood collided with the hard-light.

"Shield at 76 percent," said the voice in my ear.

"Give up yet?" asked Abigail.

The staff continued to grind on the shield, creating sparks, so I stopped pushing up and started pushing sideways, letting the stick fall beside me and into the floor. It hit the floor next to my head with a loud *POP!*

Abigail fell forward with it, giving me the chance to grab her waist and turn her around. We rolled until she was under me, the staff beside us, and her body between my knees.

She tried to get up, but I grabbed both her hands and pinned them above her head. "Give up yet?" I asked, echoing her earlier question.

"Godsdammit!" she shouted, squirming as she tried to get out of the armlock. "I had you!"

"That's twice I've pinned you now," I said, only a few centimeters from her face.

"If you're referring to the time we first met, that one didn't count. I was wearing my church garments, if you'll remember," she said.

"Fine, but that's still one to zero." I jumped to my feet, offering her my hand. "Best two out of three?"

"Deal," she said, grasping my wrist. "But I won't lose again."

As I WALKED BACK from the training area, I couldn't help but observe the sheer size of this megastructure I'd come to call "home." I could probably have fit several thousand ships the size of the *Renegade Star* inside this station, although I couldn't be sure.

I'd been here for nearly three days but still hadn't had the chance to explore much of this place. It was vast and empty but still full of passages and secrets. Given enough time, I wondered how much loot I could salvage.

I snickered as I passed through an open archway, into another corridor. This one had a garden lining its sides. Varying kinds of flowers of all colors and shapes, herbs and plants. It gave the otherwise spartan layout a bit of life, something that, for the most part, seemed to be lacking in other areas of *Titan*.

"Captain," came a voice from above. Athena instantly manifested in front of me, taking me by surprise.

"Holy hell," I said, throwing my hand up at her. "Say something before you go leaping out in front of people like that."

"I apologize," she said, bowing her head slightly. "Although I did say 'Captain.'"

I paused. Had the fancy computer program—no, the Cognitive—just given me a bit of sass? "Just tell me what you want, Athena."

She smiled pleasantly. "Yes, sir. I wanted to let you know that I have restored access to the bridge and would prefer to convene there."

"Not now," I said, fanning my hand. "I need a shower."

"Understood. When you're ready, Captain." She disappeared, fading completely out of sight.

I continued on my way, hearing laughter from further down the hall as I drew closer to the next turn.

Lex, as usual, was playing in the garden dirt, while Freddie sat nearby, reading on his pad. "Mr. Hughes!" called the little girl when she saw me.

"Hey, kid," I said, nodding.

Freddie looked up and smiled. "Back from sparring with Sister Abigail? How did the test go?"

"They're good, but there's a limit to them. We can only take so many hits before they drain." I crossed my arms. "I kicked her ass too, in case you were wondering."

"Impressive! She's quite the fighter," he said, a genuine look of astonishment on his face.

Lex held up a clump of dirt. "Mr. Hughes, you wanna play with the flowers?"

"Not particularly," I said, continuing my walk. "But you have fun in the dirt, kid."

"Thanks, Mr. Hughes!" she said, far too excited about flowers and dirt than anyone ought to be.

After leaving them, I made my way to the landing dock, where my ship, the *Renegade Star*, waited for me.

There was no one here, not since everybody moved into *Titan*. My entire crew had taken rooms that were more spacious and luxurious than the quarters they used on my ship. I couldn't say I blamed them. Besides Abigail and Lex, none of them had to bunk together anymore. They all just wanted to stretch out and relax for a change, which was only natural, but I couldn't do the same. I had to stay close to my ship, just in case.

"Welcome back, sir," said Sigmond as I entered the lounge. His voice came through the speaker system.

"Glad to be back," I muttered, heading straight to my room.

"Is there anything I can do for you, sir?"

I took my shirt off. "Start the shower, would you? I'm beat."

I stood beneath the steaming water as it hit my scalp and ran along my neck and chest. I lathered up my chest with a dab of shampoo, then closed my eyes under the flowing hot water. Over the last few weeks, I'd gone from being a lone Renegade smuggler and thief to a fugitive on an ancient megastructure searching for a mythical lost Earth, all the while being chased by two different, formerly opposed militaries that I'd somehow managed to unite against me.

If things got any more complicated, I might just have to get drunk.

Actually, now that I thought about it, that didn't sound like a terrible idea.

I turned the valve on the shower and proceeded to use the air-dryer. When I was dressed, I took my happy ass to the lounge and poured a cup of whiskey, then sat on the sofa and propped my feet up on the nearby table.

After grabbing a drink and dropping down on the sofa,

I let out a long sigh. "Aaahhh," I said. "That's what I was missing."

"Captain Hughes," said Athena. Her voice came from all around me, like she was everywhere. That was because of the artifact we'd brought with us, an old communications device known as a turn-key. I'd kept meaning to move the damn thing off this ship, but somehow it kept slipping my mind. "Captain Hughes, please respond."

"What do you want?" I asked.

"We're coming out of slipspace in fifteen minutes. Your presence is requested on the bridge."

"For what? Haven't you been managing this giant ball for two thousand years on your own? What do you need me for?"

"I believe it would be best to show you, Captain. I'll see you shortly."

"You hear that, Siggy? I can't catch a break," I said, raising my hands in frustration.

"A pity, sir," said the A.I.

"You know, Siggy," I said, getting to my feet. "Sometimes I wish it was just you and me again, out for ourselves, living the good life. All this responsibility is killing me."

"Shall I prime the engines and set a course, sir?" asked Sigmond.

I paused, thinking for a moment. "No, better not," I finally said. "Let's see where this whole thing takes us."

"As you wish, sir. I shall follow your lead."

I walked through the ship's airlock, out into the landing platform. "I'd expect nothing less, Siggy."

2

"Welcome, Captain," said Athena, who was already in her hard-light form, standing near a large monitor along the far wall.

Abigail was there too, a new outfit on and with her hair up. "Impressive, isn't it, Jace?"

"Hello to both of you," I said, having a look around. The bridge was smaller than you might imagine for a ship as large as *Titan*, but still pretty damn big. The ceiling stood at about ten meters, and there was enough space here to hold what must have been three dozen workstations.

Not that anyone used them. This entire ship was empty, except for me and my crew. It was far too much space for just eight people.

Was my crew *eight* now? Actually, I hadn't stopped to consider whether or not Camilla and her father, Bolin, qualified yet. I guessed they must, since they were here. Where else could they go? The Sarkonians and the Union would only hunt them down and try to use them as leverage against me, just like they did before.

No, I was stuck with those two, the same way I'd been stuck with Abigail, Lex, Freddie, Hitchens, and Octavia.

I smirked. Go figure. I tried going solo and it only brought me a crew.

"Not all systems are fully restored yet, I'm afraid," said the Cognitive.

"Honestly, I'm surprised this ship is still standing after…how long did you say?" asked Abigail.

"Two thousand years approximately," answered the Cognitive.

I whistled. "Long time."

"Were there many of these passengers?" asked Abigail.

"Oh, yes," the Cognitive answered. "In fact, I carried a supply of over one million inhabitants."

"A million?" I asked, dropping my jaw. "There's no way."

"Indeed, Captain. This vessel was once quite lively. Such a population could not last indefinitely, of course. Once our power core was depleted, we had no other option but to stop and begin the refueling process."

"Where did all these people go?" asked Abigail.

"To colonize," said the Cognitive. "They expanded to new worlds. Over the centuries, settlements and colonies spawned."

"No one stayed here?" I asked.

"At the time, it was impossible. The ship had lost power. Attempts were made to bring our systems back online, but the only viable solution required long-term power transference from a raw source." She waved her hand at the nearby wall, and suddenly, a screen lit up, showing the surface of the planet where we had found the moon only a few days ago. I recognized the tower and the circular building around it, except here, in this image, it was fully intact. "You saw this before, did you not?"

"Yeah, it nearly killed us," I said.

"This is but the peak of an otherwise underground structure known as a power enclave. Its purpose is to gather thermal and nuclear energy in order to resupply *Titan's* emergency power. A group of scientists and workers remained behind during the colonization effort in order to revive our systems. They were the people who built those structures. Sadly, the activation process was never performed." She smiled at me. "Until you arrived."

"In other words, they left you here to rot," I said.

"Jace, don't be rude," said Abigail, giving me a look that suggested I'd better watch myself.

I ignored her. "These people went through all the trouble of building this giant moon-sized monstrosity, only to leave it behind when it got too hard. Seems wasteful, don't you think?"

Athena didn't say anything, which told me I was right.

"Please, Captain, while I appreciate your words, I must

assure you that I was not abandoned," said Athena. "On the contrary, my mission was to deliver the colonists to their designated worlds, where they could prosper and grow. I was not able to do this, although I am happy to know the mission was ultimately a success."

The screen flickered behind her, showing the slip tunnel, and she froze for a brief moment. The tiles on the wall changed to screens, allowing us to see outside the ship. It was green and swirling, as slipspace tended to be, and lightning shattered along the distant tunnel sides.

"Exiting slipspace," said Athena, finally moving again.

A split formed before us, cutting down along the passage, revealing the dark void of normal space. *Titan* moved through it, leaving the tunnel behind. I could already see the nearby star—a small white dwarf.

Athena looked at me. "Captain, this is why I asked you to join me here. We have a situation involving our fuel reserves."

"What kind of situation?" asked another voice from behind me. I looked to see Freddie standing next to the door.

"What are you doing here?" asked Abigail.

"I was hoping to ask Athena something, but it can wait," he said.

I turned back to Athena. "You heard the man. Let's hear it."

The Cognitive nodded. "*Titan*'s fuel core is based on tritium, an extremely rare compound not easily manufactured. Because of this, *Titan* was outfitted with several other reserve systems, including solar. If we are to continue our voyage to Earth, we will require frequent refueling, due to the consumption requirements of slip-space travel."

"How frequent?" asked Freddie.

"For every hour of slipspace travel, we will need six hours of refueling," explained Athena.

I scoffed. "Are you kidding? Why the hell can't you just use a regular slipspace generator?"

"*Titan* creates its own tunnels," said Athena. "In order to do so, a great deal of energy is required. We could traverse pre-existing tunnels, of course, but we are currently nowhere near any established pathways."

"We're not near any tunnels?" I asked.

"When we escaped from your pursuers—General Marcus Brigham and the Sarkonians, was it?"

I nodded. "Bunch of bastards."

"Indeed," she continued. "When we formed a new tunnel, it took us out of the previously established network. We will need to reestablish our path if we plan to use existing tunnels in the future. The alternative is constant refueling."

"If we kept refueling, how long would it take to get to Earth?" asked Freddie.

She froze in place for a second, then blinked. "Twenty-six years, five months, and twenty-three days."

"Damn," I muttered. "Guess we can't do that."

"We can," she corrected. "However, you will have aged a great deal."

Freddie gulped. "I'd be in my fifties."

I glared at him. "Right, so we're not doing that. You said the only other option is using the existing tunnel network?"

She ran a finger along the wall and it changed, showing a single blue dot at the center. "This is our current position," she said.

A few other dots appeared around the blue one. A moment later, thousands more came into view, creating what I immediately realized was a galaxy.

"You'll notice where we are, but observe," she said, snapping her fingers.

A line formed, expanding from our blue dot to another yellow dot, then another. It branched into three, continued in multiple directions.

"The network grows and breaks at various points, but there is usually a through-line, connecting everything in one way or another. It appears complicated, but observe." She snapped her fingers again, and this time, a single blue line appeared, beginning with our position and ending somewhere on the other side of the galaxy. It zigzagged in various directions, yet never broke. "The problem now, of course, is how long it will take. Even with this particular path, our flight time is still rather long."

"Not twenty-six years, though," said Freddie.

"Correct. This path is much shorter, requiring sixty-seven tunnels and over five years of travel time."

"Five years?" I asked, not hiding my frustration. "I'm not sure I can stay cramped up on this moon for that long."

She nodded. "I understand it is not ideal, which is why I have prepared a third solution, should you wish to hear it. I must tell you, however, that it is more dangerous than the other two."

"Let's hear it. I like to know my options before I commit to anything."

She flicked her wrist, causing the screen to zoom in on part of the galaxy, directly in the existing path of the blue line. "There is a planet, not far from our present location, that I believe contains another tritium core."

"You should have led with that," I said. "Could've saved me ten minutes better spent sleeping and drinking."

"Apologies," she said. "There is a problem with the location, which is why I waited to provide the option."

"What's wrong with this one?" asked Freddie.

"The map you provided allowed me to analyze the borders of the various governmental bodies. Based on that information, it would seem this planet exists within the Union's territory, making it difficult to access."

I sighed. "That's why you didn't tell me right away."

"Correct. I also believe this planet has been colonized, which means the core may be difficult to obtain."

"What's this world called?" Freddie asked.

"Unknown," said Athena. "There was no information in the media provided, aside from its location."

"None whatsoever?" asked Freddie. "That's unusual. Don't you think so, Captain? Have you ever seen anything like that before?"

"I've seen classified ships and military bases on moons that shouldn't be there, but never a planet without a name." I turned back to Athena. "So our options are twenty-six years of stop-and-go refuelings, five years of following the slip tunnel network, or stealing a new core from inside Union space. Sounds like three lousy scenarios, if you ask me."

Freddie nodded in agreement. "I don't think attacking a colony is worth the risk. We're free of both the Union and the Sarkonians right now. They'll have a hard time keeping up with us if we just keep going."

"Possibly," said Athena.

"Possibly?" I repeated. "What does *that* mean?"

"The tunnels we form remain accessible to others once we create them," she explained.

I raised my brow. "Come again? Did you just say the tunnels don't close behind us?"

"Wait, does this mean the Union might be following us?" asked Freddie.

"Should your pursuers decide to continue after us, it will be impossible to stay ahead of them indefinitely. Our rate of attrition is simply too great," said Athena.

"All because we keep stopping for fuel?" I asked.

"Correct," said Athena. "Following the existing slip-space network will allow us to preserve a great deal of that fuel, but not all of it. We will need to stop again eventually, and when that happens, I will be unable to ensure our safety."

"Have you picked up any ships behind us?" I asked.

"None so far," she assured me. "However, that could change at any moment."

I tried to weigh my options, but each one seemed like too much of a risk. If we kept going, we risked letting the Union find us. After that, it'd be a dice roll to see if we had the energy reserves to use *Titan*'s shields.

"What should we do, Captain?" asked Freddie.

"Gather the crew," I told him. "We'll need to figure this out together before we make that decision. Tell everyone to meet me in the conference room."

3

Rather than head straight there, I decided to make a quick stop in Alphonse's room. If anyone could give me some insight on the Union's thought process, it would be a Constable.

"Ah, Captain Hughes," said Alphonse, when he saw the door open. He sat in his bed, reading a pad. Octavia had given him a digital library of over six thousand books. A kinder gesture than I would've done, but then, he did save Lex from being kidnapped, so maybe we owed him.

I still wasn't sure how I felt about Alphonse. Not yet. There was a strong possibility that he was playing all of us, that killing Docker to save Lex was all a show, and that eventually he'd find a way to take us all out. You might have thought I was paranoid, but when you're a Renegade, that kind of thinking keeps you alive. It'd worked for me so far.

"Constable," I said, holding my pistol at my hip. I shut the door behind me, never letting him out of my sights. "I've come to have a talk."

"I thought you might, given our last discussion," he said, setting down the pad.

"Sorry to interrupt your reading." I didn't move any closer, just kept my distance, staying near the door. The way I'd heard it, Constables were fast and deadly. I'd never met one before Alphonse, but I wasn't taking any chances.

He smirked. "Octavia provided me with some fascinating reading material. All fiction, except most of it is...how shall I put this?" He paused, glancing at the pad. "I suppose it's a bit...erotic."

"Erotic?" I asked.

"Perhaps she thought it would be funny," he said, looking genuinely amused. "In any case, I've been reading one of the least graphic ones about two soldiers—one Union and one Sarkonian—who fall in love, only to have their respective governments go after them. I have to say, despite the suggestive nature of it, the politics of the story are actually fairly well-developed. I suspect the writer, Lucy Valentine, though clearly a penname, must have some former experience with government work."

"Sounds like you're just bored," I said.

"There is that," he said, nodding. "Yet another reason I am glad to see you."

"Speaking of," I said. "Let's get to why I'm here."

He leaned forward. "Do tell."

I glanced in the corner of the room, where I knew there was a camera. I'd asked Athena to let us use this particular location so that we could keep a better eye on Alphonse. I suspected he knew this, although I couldn't be sure.

I held my hand to my ear, pretending like I was speaking into a communication device. "Athena, show the planet we discussed earlier," I said.

The wall to my left changed at once, showing a world with dozens of continents.

"Do you know where this is?" I asked, looking at Alphonse.

He got to his feet and, with his hands behind his back, slowly approached the display. "It looks familiar. Where is this located?"

"Inside Union space," I said.

He touched his chin, nodding slowly. "I see…and the name of the planet?"

"It's not listed," I said. "But something tells me you already knew that."

He cracked a smile. "I like your faith in me, Captain."

"I wouldn't go that far. I just expect a Constable to know a thing or two about unlisted worlds. Am I wrong?"

"Priscilla," he said, crossing his leg. "The name of that planet is Priscilla."

I chewed on that for a moment, concluding that it was a stupid name to give a planet and rather something you might call a three-year-old girl with pigtails.

"Why isn't its name listed in the database?" I asked.

"The same reason that you're interested in it," said Alphonse. "At least, that's my assumption. Tell me, Captain, are you after an artifact? Is that what this is all about?"

"What do you know about it?" I asked him.

"Not as much as you, I'm guessing, but enough to know it's priceless."

"It's nothing for you to be concerned with," I said.

He chuckled. "No, I don't suppose it is, given my current situation."

"Got anything else you can tell me about this Priscilla?" I asked.

"Only that you should keep your distance," said Alphonse.

"Oh? Why's that?"

He cleared his throat. "First, there's something you should know."

"Is this where you tell me a story, Al?" I asked.

He smiled, ignoring my sarcasm, and continued. "The Constables, on average, receive more intelligence than any governmental body in the entire Union. I've seen reports on things that you couldn't possibly imagine, much of which is located on Priscilla, buried underground in the vaults. Priscilla is the Union's dumping ground for all exotic artifacts that the government believes to be of any significance."

"Are you telling me that planet is some sort of Union warehouse full of priceless artifacts?" I asked.

"Not entirely. There's more to the galaxy than relics

from Earth, but yes, I suspect you will find a great many things of value on Priscilla," he said. "That is, if you can take them without getting killed."

"Don't you worry about me," I told him.

"But I do, Captain, which is why I'm going to offer you my services, should you require them," said Alphonse.

"That's the other half of why I'm here, Constable. I need to know how far your access goes," I explained.

"Are you asking if I have the ability to enter the facility on Priscilla?" he asked.

"That's right," I said.

"I have a level-10 clearance. It can take me as far as the lowest floor of the main lab."

"Isn't that as far as we need to be?" I asked.

Alphonse shook his head. "No, not quite."

"What else is left?" I asked.

"There's a door," he said. "A very large door. Behind that, you'll find what you're after. Only two people have access. The lead researcher and the commander in charge of the base. Your best bet would be the researcher. Of course, this is all contingent on you reaching that point."

"You don't think we can do it?" I asked.

"On the contrary, Captain. I have full faith in your capabilities. It's just that you've never tried to pretend you're a Constable. They'll ask you a series of questions that you won't be able to answer. They might decide to run your face through the database." He sighed. "And that's just you. If you bring any of your accomplices, they won't have an I.D."

Godsdammit, I thought. The way he made it sound, getting caught seemed inevitable.

"Might I propose another solution?" he asked.

"Depends," I said. "If you're asking to leave this cell, I'm afraid I can't oblige."

"That's too bad," he said with a frown. "I was only going to say that the best means you have of retrieving what you need is to take me with you."

I scoffed. "No way in hell am I doing that," I snapped.

"I'm afraid it's your best option," he said. "The security detail that meets you will want to see me standing with you. I've been there before and they know my face. At least, their head researcher does, Doctor MaryAnn Dressler. There's always a chance she won't be there to meet you, but given the unexpectedness of your arrival, it seems likely she'll want to know why you're…why *I'm* there."

He had a point, but I wasn't about to tell him that. Alphonse was a Constable. How could I trust a man like that, even if he did save Lex from a would-be kidnapper? The man could be hiding something, and I was certain he was, but I also had to get into that base and take that core, one way or another.

No, I couldn't do it. I couldn't walk into that facility with a Constable beside me.

Could I?

"Piss off, Al," I said, hitting the door control and stepping out into the hall. "I'm not letting you out of here."

"That's too bad," he said, then gave me a soft smile.

The door began to close as I lowered my gun, still watching him.

He picked up his pad and tapped the screen. "Good luck on Priscilla," he said, leaning back on the bed and crossing his feet. "I'll be here if you need me."

4

"THAT'S CRAZY," said Octavia. She sat in her chair at the end of the conference table.

"Which part?" I asked from the opposite end. "There was a lot to unpack."

Abigail, Hitchens, Freddie, and Bolin had taken seats along each side, listening intently.

"The part where you suggested we fly into Union space and steal a power core from a government facility," she responded.

"Oh, that," I said, fanning my hand. "Yeah, I guess it's a bit messy."

"More than a bit," muttered Abigail.

"It's the only option we have, unless you're all okay with sitting on this ship for the next five years, just hoping the Union doesn't catch up to us," I said.

"We can't do that either," said Freddie.

"So how's this going to work?" asked Octavia. "You sneak in and steal the core? What about security?"

"You're talking about if we get caught," I said.

"Won't you?" she asked.

"Probably," I conceded. "I just don't see any other way around it."

"What about Alphonse?" asked Octavia. "You said he offered to go with you."

"We can't do that!" said Freddie.

"Why not?" asked Octavia.

"Isn't it obvious?" he asked. "He works for the Union!"

"Not anymore. Besides, he saved Lex and has been providing Captain Hughes with valuable intelligence. Did you already forget about the cloak?" she asked.

"What do you mean?" asked Freddie.

I cleared my throat. "Alphonse told me how Brigham was tracking us. He's the reason we managed to escape when we did."

"Even still," interjected Abigail. "He's not to be trusted. We have no idea what his true motivation is."

I thought about it for a second. Both Abigail and Octavia were right. We couldn't trust Alphonse, even if we wanted to, but we still needed him. I'd known it when I was talking to him in his room, and I knew it right now.

"Are you suggesting we hold a gun to his head?" asked Freddie.

"Why not?" asked Abigail.

"I don't think they'll let you carry a weapon into Priscilla just so you can keep Alphonse in check," said Octavia. "You're going to need a better way."

"There might be a way around that," I finally said. "We could put a bomb on him. If he tries anything—" I raised my fist and extended my fingers, like an explosion. "—no more Constable."

Freddie's eyes widened. "S-seriously?"

"Do we have that kind of device?" asked Octavia, apparently not fazed by my morbid suggestion.

"That's where Athena comes in," I said.

"Hello," said Athena, suddenly appearing behind Bolin and Hitchens.

"Goodness!" exclaimed Hitchens, clutching his chest.

"I apologize," said the Cognitive. "I sometimes forget that sudden appearances can be alarming to humans."

"Don't worry about it," I said, fanning my hand at Hitchens. "He's fine. Now, Athena, you think you can help us out with Alphonse?"

"Your proposal is possible, although dangerous and highly unethical," she said. "I must admit I have reservations."

"That's an average day for us," I said, unwrapping a piece of hard candy—strawberry flavored—and stuffed the treat in my mouth.

Hitchens twisted his lips. "Would it be possible to use those tractor beams to pull the object out from within the compound?"

Athena frowned. "The tractor beam cannot reach the surface of a planet from space. It would have to be much closer. Besides, we currently lack the necessary power needed. I also fear doing so would deplete what little energy reserves we have upon our arrival."

"That's a shame," he said.

"Indeed, it is," said Athena.

"Guess that just leaves one option," I said, thumbing the side of the desk. "Which means the next problem is getting around their security. Most of us are on the Union's watch list. We'll have to find a way to mask our identities."

"How do we do that?" asked Hitchens.

I shook my head. "Beats me." For once, I was out of solutions.

"You can use the personal shields," said Athena.

The suggestion took me by surprise. "The shields?"

"I can modify them to alter your appearance, although you'll have to be careful not to let anyone touch you," said the Cognitive.

"You can do that?" asked Abby.

The artificial woman smiled. "I will need some time to make the necessary modifications, but I believe I can accommodate your request."

"This is crazy," muttered Freddie. "We're talking about sending the two of you down there alone with a Constable, disguised with ancient technology, all so you can steal an artifact from what must be one of the most heavily guarded vaults in Union space."

"Your point?" I asked.

He blinked at me, then shook his head. "Oh, never mind."

I gave a slight shrug. "It'll be fine, Fred."

"Because that makes it better," he said.

"How can we be certain that Alphonse is telling the truth?" asked Abigail. "What if we get down there and it turns out he can't even get through the front door?"

"We'll handle it," I said, more than confident in my ability to get the hell out of a bad situation. "If worse comes to worst, we'll blow up the whole godsdamn building."

"It's always explosions with you," she said.

"You're the one who used my quad cannon to drop a crater in the middle of Spiketown," I countered. "Or did you forget about that?"

She gave me a wry smile.

Bolin, who had been quiet until now, leaned on the table with his elbow. "What can the rest of us do?"

"Stay on *Titan* and protect what matters," I said. "If we fail, then you go with the second option. Run and hide."

Everyone was quiet for a moment as my words lingered in the air. "You can't do this alone," said Freddie. "I'm coming with you."

I shook my head. "Don't be ridiculous. We can't risk too many people on this job. We're already pushing it with the two of us."

"You don't think I can be of use?" he asked.

"No, I just think you need more training before you're ready for this." I looked at Abigail. "You agree?"

She glanced at Freddie then nodded. "It needs to be a small team. The fewer, the better."

"Jace is right," muttered Octavia. "We have to trust these two to get the job done. They always do."

Abigail raised her head at Athena. "Can we take another look in that armory of yours?"

"By all means," said the Cognitive. "I'll be happy to assist you."

I LINGERED BEHIND after the meeting, when I noticed Freddie meandering in the corner. He seemed to be lost in thought, staring blankly at the floor.

I already knew the reason. He wanted to help, the same way he always did. He'd made improvements since I'd first met him, even getting his first kill, but it wasn't enough to warrant this kind of mission. He still had a long way to go.

"Fred?" I said, tapping his arm.

"Huh?" he said, blinking. "Oh, sorry, Captain."

"What's the problem?" I asked.

"I'm just thinking," he said.

"About?"

He hesitated to answer. "Nothing important. I still need to talk to Athena about a request I had."

"Oh, yeah," I said, remembering what he'd said when I

ran into him on the bridge. "Didn't you take care of it yet?"

Athena appeared beside me. "You needed to speak with me, Frederick?"

Freddie jumped, taken by surprise. "Ah!"

I chuckled. "Well, go on and ask her. She's eager to find out."

"I, uh," he began. "I was hoping you'd have something to help me improve my skillset, Athena. A training program, if possible."

"What sort of skillset?" asked the Cognitive.

"I think Freddie wants you to help him learn how to kill people," I said plainly.

Freddie's eyes widened. "Captain! I didn't mean it like that."

"Sure you did," I said. "Don't try to walk around it. Say what you mean, kid. It'll save you more time than you realize."

"I believe I understand," said Athena. "Frederick, can you please join me in Section 018 of Deck 04?"

He nodded quickly. "I'll be right there!"

She vanished. "Very well," said her disembodied voice. "I shall see you soon."

"Wonder what she's going to teach you," I said, scratching my ear.

"Me too," said Freddie. He started to leave. "I'll let you know how it goes!"

"Sure thing," I said, watching him take off down the hall. "Just don't do anything stupid."

5

ABIGAIL and I met in the armory, hoping to be fully prepared for the mission ahead. I was already planning to pick up some shields, but I still hadn't had time to browse the entire inventory yet. I needed to prepare for the possibility of us ending up in a firefight, should the plan go belly-up.

Hell, who was I kidding? We were heading straight into one of the most heavily guarded facilities in Union space. A simple firefight was the least of my worries.

"Okay, Abby," I said to her as we walked in between two rows of lockers. "What are we looking for?"

"Guns," she said. "What else?"

"I don't know what other answer I expected," I admitted. "Athena! You there?"

The Cognitive appeared a few meters in front of us. "Welcome. I have a few items set aside for your consideration, if you'll follow me."

She turned and started walking to the far wall in the back of the room. We followed, passing by dozens of sealed lockers. I wondered what was in each of these and why we were passing them by.

I decided to wait and see what she had for us before I bothered with questions.

Athena brought Abby and me to a large table with several items placed neatly across the surface. I recognized a few instantly, including the shield modules we'd trained with earlier today. No sign of the electric staffs, though. "Each of these items has been specially chosen to aid you in your mission," said the Cognitive. "There are better weapons, but due to your limited biology, you will be unable to wield them."

"Limited biology?" I asked.

"She means we don't have Lex's markings," said Athena.

Right, of course, I thought. Since I'd arrived on *Titan,* I noticed I couldn't interact with certain devices, including locked doors and passages. Athena had to let me in, and sometimes it was a problem. The bridge, for example, couldn't be accessed without Athena's permission, although Lex had no problem getting inside on her own. The same was true of the armory as well as the upper decks. "What are we working with?" I asked.

"Lighter small arms," informed Athena. "Here we have the AD-619 as well as the SS-223. Both are capable of single and burst firing. The bullets are refined carbon fiber ammunitions, strong enough to pierce most industrial metals, while also resisting most scans and inspection devices, although I am basing that assumption on your ship's database."

"So you're not sure," I said.

"The material used to create all of this equipment requires advanced detection abilities, which I do not believe the Union possesses. However, given the blackout of information surrounding your target facility, I cannot be certain," explained Athena.

"If things go bad, we'll just kill everybody," said Abigail.

"That's the spirit," I said, taking the pistol. I turned it over in my hand, feeling the weight. It was exceptionally well-balanced, better than my standard pistol, and the grip was smooth and comfortable, like it had been custom made for my hand. "Not bad," I said.

"Next, you'll recognize your shields. They are fully charged and can withstand multiple direct hits. I suggest using caution, nonetheless, as they will degrade with enough use. Additionally, you'll find they've been modified with alternate identities to assist you in the mission."

Abigail picked up the shield and placed it on her shoulder. It glowed briefly with a soft green, then disappeared, blending in with her skin. I was about to ask when it was supposed to start working, when Abigail's face suddenly changed. Her eyes grew slightly thinner, changing from green to brown, her hair turned black, and her skin color was a few shades darker.

I blinked, surprised by how drastic the change had been.

"What is it?" she asked, noticing my expression.

My mouth dropped when I heard her voice. It sounded different, raspier. "Holy shit," I finally said.

"What?" she asked again, looking at Athena. "Is it broken?"

Athena snapped her fingers and the wall behind her changed, showing Abigail's new body. "Your new design, Ms. Pryar."

Abigail gawked at her new appearance then glanced at her arms, twisting them to get a better look at her body. She bent her ass, trying to see her hips and legs. "Not bad," she said.

I grabbed the other shield and snapped it to my shoulder. "Let's see what I'm working with," I said.

I saw a brief flicker of blue in my eyes, but nothing seemed to happen. "Did it work?" I asked, looking at my hands. They looked pretty similar to my old set.

Abigail covered her mouth, giggling.

"What's so funny?" I asked.

"You look...different," she said after a second.

"Athena, let me see," I said.

Athena flicked her fingers again and the screen

changed, showing a tall man with white hair and bags under his eyes. No, they were wrinkles. He was old. Too old, godsdammit.

Abigail laughed. "You're a grandfather!"

"Athena!" I barked. "What's the deal?"

"Your disguise," the Cognitive explained.

"I look like I'm about to keel over," I said.

"Considering that you are attempting to hide your identity, is this *not* the best solution?" asked Athena. "You look nothing like your normal self."

"She's right," said Abigail. "Good work, Athena."

"Thank you, Ms. Pryar," said the Cognitive, smiling. "I am glad you approve."

"Enemies, all around me," I said, shaking my head. I felt around my arm, locating the device and turning it off. The display behind Athena switched off right when I pressed the button, reverting the wall back to the way it looked before. "What's next on the list?" I scanned the table and noticed a small rectangular box. "Looks like a present."

Athena took the lid off the small case and set it a few centimeters from the box. Inside, I spotted a small stick about thirty centimeters in length. She picked it up and carefully handed it to Abigail.

The former nun took it curiously, but I could tell she had no idea what it was or what to do with it.

"Please touch the white notch on the bottom," said Athena.

Abigail turned the stick in her hand and found the spot, then touched her index finger to it.

A sudden shock sparked on the opposite end, startling her. "Whoa!" she exclaimed.

"Hey, easy," I said, taking a step back.

"Yes, please use caution," agreed Athena. "This is a miniaturized version of the staff you requested this morning. I chose this because it can be more easily concealed." She reached over to Abigail, wrapping her fingers around the electric half of the object. The sparks went straight through her hand. "Also, if you'll just twist here…"

She turned the stick and released it, letting the other half extend outward until it was full length.

Abigail was so surprised, she nearly dropped it.

At this size, it resembled a baton, roughly one meter in length. Still smaller than the staff from this morning, but maybe even more useful, considering we'd be in a building, maneuvering through tighter spaces.

"I would advise you to extend the device before activating the electric current," said the Cognitive.

"I see," muttered Abigail. She raised the baton, examining the light on the other end, then brought the weapon down against the floor, letting out a sharp boom. It echoed through the open armory, taking us both by surprise. Abigail grinned. "Interesting."

"I'm glad you approve," said Athena. "Captain, shall I retrieve another for you?"

I glanced at the stick then shook my head. "I'll take a pistol over whatever that is any day of the week."

"Your loss," said Abigail.

"Once we have *Titan* at full capacity, I assure you our armaments will be greatly improved," said Athena. "That is only one of many reasons we must retrieve the tritium core."

"I think we can handle it," said Abigail, turning off the electric charge and compressing the stick to its normal size. "Don't you agree, Jace?"

"You're asking me if I think we can pull off a heist?" I asked, giving her a sly grin. "Don't worry, ladies. I was born with a lockpick in my hand. That core is as good as ours."

I took an elevator to get back to the deck where my ship was waiting. As soon as the doors opened, I heard someone laughing from down the hall.

It was Lex, chasing Bolin's daughter, Camilla. "Can't catch me!" shouted the older girl. She laughed as Lex trailed behind her.

Lex giggled as the two came towards me, almost plowing straight into my hip, when I managed to step aside. "Whoa there!" I said.

Lex stopped, huffing and puffing, out of breath. "Sorry, Mr. Hughes!"

"You kids having fun out here?" I asked.

"We're exploring," said Lex.

I looked at Camilla. "That right?"

The older girl nodded. "Lex can get us into all the rooms, so we decided to see what else we could find."

"That's fine, but make sure you don't leave this deck," I said. "We still haven't explored the upper floors or anything. I can't have either of you accidentally wandering into an airlock."

They both looked at each other. "An airlock?!" said Camilla, suddenly terrified.

"Yep, you better be careful. There's places around here that are sealed for a reason."

Lex gulped. "Really?"

"Yeah, but don't worry, kid. Just stick to this deck and be careful. Camilla will look after you," I said, looking at the other girl. "Right?"

Camilla ran up and took Lex's hand. "Right. I won't let anything happen to you, Lex. I promise."

Lex smiled.

I watched the two of them run back into the hall and take the next turn, heading toward the cafeteria. *Crisis averted*, I thought. The last thing anyone needed was for those two to get themselves lost, not that I expected that to happen with Athena around.

But still, I'd only been here for three days. It was hardly enough time to explore every nook and cranny.

For all I knew, Lex's tattoos might lead her to a bomb

with enough firepower to wipe out a small planet. Who knew what sort of crazy crap this moon had hiding on it?

Regardless, I had my work cut out for me tomorrow. If I expected to be at my peak, I'd need a few drinks and a hard sleep.

Time to get to it.

6

SOMEDAY, *you're gonna learn, Jacey…what it means to be a man*, I heard a voice say. *Someday, you're gonna know…what it feels like to be me…*

My eyes snapped open, and it took me a moment to realize where I was, here in my bed. I wiped my arm against my forehead and cheek, trying to clear off the sweat. "Gods," I muttered, licking my chapped lips and swallowing.

I sat up, foggy-headed, feeling like I was hung over. I glanced at the table and saw a half-empty bottle of whiskey.

Guess that explains it, I thought.

"Good morning, sir," said Sigmond. "Is there anything I can do for you?"

"What's the status of *Titan* right now?" I asked.

"Athena has informed me that we are nearly at our

destination," explained the A.I. "We should arrive in under two hours."

I contemplated going back to sleep to try and get rid of this hangover but decided against it. Instead, I went for my cabinet and grabbed one of my remaining pills. Polynex, used for headaches and dehydration. I took it with two glasses of water.

The meds took effect when I was halfway through my shower. It felt like a weight had been lifted off my chest.

By the time I was dressed, I felt completely reenergized.

"Siggy, tell Octavia to meet me at Alphonse's cell."

"Understood, sir," said Sigmond.

I grabbed a protein bar from the cabinet and scarfed it down in record time, following it up with a swig from my water jug. That would tide me over for a while. My time as a Renegade had taught me never to eat too much before or after a job. Your nerves can't handle it, and the last thing you want when you're deep in it is to lose your lunch.

That was the thing about this line of work. When the adrenaline kicked in, you had to be ready for it, and having a routine was good for that.

I moved quickly through the landing bay and into the hall, rounding the corner to the elevator. It took me straight up to the deck where we had stashed Alphonse.

To my surprise, Octavia was already there waiting for me. "Took your time, didn't you?" she asked a second after the elevator doors opened.

I stared at her for a second, wondering how someone in

a wheelchair could move so fast. "Mind your business, lady."

"Are you ready to handle this?" she asked, ignoring my statement.

I walked forward, stopping beside her, just before Alphonse's door. "I'm always ready," I said, glancing down.

"If he tries anything,.."

"I'll kill him," I said.

She nodded. "Only if he misbehaves."

"We'll see," I said, winking.

Alphonse was standing beside his bed when I entered, his shirt off and Athena's hand inside of his stomach.

"Uh," I muttered, looking at them both. "What in holy hell did I just walk in on?"

Athena pulled her hand back, removing it from the Constable's abdomen. "Apologies," she said. "I was placing the device."

"The bomb," he said, matter-of-factly.

"It went well, I take it?" I asked.

Alphonse looked at Athena. "I'm not sure. Did it?"

"It was as you requested, Captain Hughes," said Athena.

"Good," I said. "If you try anything between now and when we're back in this room, we'll blow your ass to bits. You hear what I'm telling you?"

"I do," he said.

I holstered my pistol but kept my eye on him as we moved into the hall. Octavia sat in her chair, still in the same position. "Constable," she said, tipping her head to him.

"Ms. Brie," he said, returning the nod.

"You two behave yourselves," she said.

I flicked my finger up in the shape of a pistol as I passed. "Enjoy sitting around."

"Funny," she said right as we walked into the elevator.

The doors closed as she shot me a thin smile.

Alphonse leaned against the wall as we rode the lift to the lower deck, where my ship waited. "I hope you have a plan to conceal your identity when we—"

"Don't worry about me," I said, giving him a look. "Just don't screw any of this up."

"If I do, we're both dead," he said, then placed his hand on his stomach. "Me more than you, probably."

He didn't seem to be scared or excited, only calm and collected, the way I imagined a Constable would be. Alphonse, for all the distrust I had of him, was definitely something else.

We arrived in the bay and made our way into my ship. Abigail was already inside, holding her rifle and sitting on the couch. "It's about time," she said when she saw me, immediately getting to her feet.

"Sorry to keep you waiting," said Alphonse.

"Don't apologize to the nun," I said. "Siggy, prep the engines. Alphonse, take a seat."

"Understood, sir," responded Sigmond.

"Should we expect any trouble from you?" Abigail asked, staring at the Constable.

"Don't worry about him," I said. "Come with me to the cockpit, Abby."

"You're going to leave him out here alone?" she asked.

"What's he going to do?" I asked. "If he doesn't follow orders, he'll explode."

"And I really don't want to explode," said Alphonse.

"See? Now let's go," I said, grabbing her hand.

She followed me to the front of the ship, and I closed the door behind us. "What's wrong?" she asked, leaning in close, like she expected me to tell her some big secret.

I shrugged and flopped down in my chair. "Nothing," I answered, then reached beneath the console and pulled out a bottle of whiskey, along with two glasses. "I just wanted to have a drink."

"A drink? Are you seriously going to—"

"I have one before every job. It's part of how I operate. You gonna lecture me or join?"

"Don't you think it's a bad idea to do that before an operation?"

"That's your problem, Abby," I said, pouring a small shot's worth of liquor into both glasses. "You're calling this an operation. You're too uptight."

I offered up the cup to her and she stared at it. "Fine," she said after a short moment. "But only one."

I grinned. "That's a good nun."

"I told you to stop calling me a nun," she said, glaring a little.

We clinked the glasses together, and I raised mine in the air. "Here's to…" I paused, trying to think of something.

"To us," she said, holding up her own glass.

I smiled. "A couple of fools inside a ship inside a moon inside a slip tunnel."

We touched our cups together, then shot the drinks back. It burned, but we didn't complain.

"Another?" I asked.

She fanned her hand. "Not now. Later, once we're done."

I nodded, setting down the empty glass. "Once we're done."

TITAN LEFT the tunnel and entered the Navi system. It was largely empty, just inside Union territory. From here, we'd take the *Renegade Star* and hop through another tunnel to reach Priscilla.

Titan, meanwhile, would create a new tunnel to Priscilla, staying inside until a certain amount of time had passed. At that point, the moon would emerge, pick us up, and get the hell out of there before the entire godsdamn Union fleet arrived.

Athena had suggested I load my ship with some specialized proximity mines. I had rejected them at first, since I had no experience using them. After some insistence on her part, I decided to go along with it.

After the old mines had been swapped with the new ones, I decided to relax in my ship until it was time to go.

"We all set?" I asked, sitting in the cockpit, prepped to depart.

Abigail was beside me, suited up in plated armor, blonde hair in a ponytail, and a rifle at her side. She looked like a warrior woman, built to kill.

I had to admit, I liked it.

"*Renegade Star*, you are clear for departure," said Athena, over my com.

"There's your answer," said Abby, motioning with her hand.

"If you're ready, I'm ready," I said.

"One question. How do we know when and where to meet *Titan* once we're away from the planet?" Abigail asked.

"Sigmond has the info," I said, gripping the controls. I felt the engine ignite, lifting us off the deck. The ship vibrated for a moment, until the stabilizers kicked in.

"That is correct," said Siggy. "Athena's arrival at Priscilla should occur approximately two hours after we land on the planet. You will need to be back aboard this vessel several minutes before that time."

"Two hours to steal the core?" asked Abigail. "Is that enough time?"

"It has to be," I said, pushing the control stick and

bringing the ship out of the deck. "*Titan* doesn't have the energy reserves to stay in slipspace for long. That's what Athena tells me anyway."

"That is correct," confirmed Athena. "It is essential that you deliver the tritium core before my fuel reserves are depleted."

"No pressure," I told Abby.

The *Renegade Star* pushed out of *Titan*'s landing bay and into open space. A few moments later, *Titan* let out a large beam, splitting open a tear in space, creating a new slip tunnel.

We entered first, with the moon-sized megastructure following closely behind.

IT ONLY TOOK ten minutes to reach the other end of the tunnel. We were alone when we emerged. Despite knowing what would happen, I was still surprised that *Titan* didn't follow. Despite Athena telling me it wouldn't, I had never witnessed a ship enter slipspace but not emerge. Whatever *Titan* was made of, whatever technology its ancient engineers had used to create it, there could be no argument that it was a marvel.

"We have arrived at our destination," said Sigmond. "Proceeding to Priscilla."

"Aside from what we're after, do you think this facility has anything else worth taking?" asked Abigail.

"I've been wondering about that too," I admitted. "We won't know until we're inside. Our job is to steal the core, but maybe we'll get lucky and bag ourselves a second prize."

"I'll keep my fingers crossed for something nice," she said, giving me a wink.

The gesture took me by surprise. Was she flirting with me? Was she joking? I shook it off and buried the question. *Get your head in the game, Jace.*

The holo lit up on the console, showing the planet and our route. The landing site was close to the coast of the largest continent, maybe twenty kilometers away from the sea. We'd be landing there in under five minutes.

"Right," she said, leaning closer to the floating planet on the dash.

"That's not to say we can't steal a few extras while we're there," I added with a smirk. I thumbed the Foxy Stardust bobblehead. "You never know what you'll find when you go thieving."

We entered the planet's orbit, positioning ourselves to land. The process wouldn't take long. Maybe eight minutes.

As we proceeded toward the facility, a voice came over the com. "Incoming vessel, please identify yourself."

I tabbed the console, opening the line. "This is Constable Alphonse Malloy, requesting permission to land."

"C-constable, did you say?" asked the person on the other end.

"That's right," I answered. "I'm here to perform a surprise inspection. My authorization code is 66192-883."

A short pause.

"Authorization code accepted. Welcome to Priscilla, sir."

I smiled right as we broke through the clouds, then turned the com off and looked at Abigail. "Ready to be someone else?"

She picked up her rifle then slapped her shield onto her shoulder. With a soft click, a blue glow appeared around her, instantly transforming her face and body. "Ready," she confirmed.

I followed suit, activating my shield just as the *Renegade Star* set down on the landing pad. I glanced at the reflective glass to my left side, spotting my silver hair in the display. "Okay," I said, glancing back at Abby. "Let's go steal us a power core."

7

FOUR MEN with guns met us at the landing pad, each dressed in a Union military uniform. Behind them, a woman with glasses walked with a serious expression. She had short, black hair and a slender frame. If it hadn't been for the scowl, I might've found her attractive.

Okay, even with the scowl.

"Welcome to Priscilla," said the woman in a thick accent I didn't recognize. "My name is Doctor Dressler. I've been informed that you're here to perform an inspection. Is that right?"

"It is," said Alphonse, giving her a pleasant smile. "I apologize for our impromptu arrival, but my superiors wanted a confirmation assessment on the property."

Dressler looked at her pad then at each of us. "May I

ask," she went on, "who are your associates? They don't appear in our registry."

"Constables," said Alphonse flatly. "Their identities are masked, due to their recent assignments." He gestured to me then to Abby. "I take responsibility for both of them. That is all you need to know."

"Be that as it may, I will have to ask that they relinquish their weapons until the end of the inspection. It's a matter of protocol."

Alphonse looked at me, and I gave him a slight nod. "Very well," said the Constable.

Both Abigail and I gave up our two primary weapons but didn't mention anything about the pistols we received from *Titan*, which remained concealed beneath our clothes.

"Shall we proceed with the inspection?" asked Alphonse. "I have other matters to attend to and would prefer to keep this brief."

"Brief?" asked Dressler.

"I don't expect to uncover anything unusual. Your facility is one of the best, Doctor."

"Thank you," she said, nodding. "Please follow me. I'll be happy to show you the grounds."

Alphonse started walking and both Abigail and I quickly followed. The Union soldiers remained behind us, trailing until we entered the front of the main building. They didn't join us, which suggested we were in the clear.

As soon as we entered, a man behind a small counter rose to his feet. He asked Alphonse to press his thumb to a small, flat device. The Constable did, and a green light beeped. "Clear," the man said.

That must have been the blood test, I thought.

The retinal scan came next, just inside the next hall. Alphonse bent forward and a blue line swept across his face. "Identity confirmed," said the facility's A.I.

Abby and I proceeded through the door, right after him. When we were finally through the short series of identity tests, the doctor turned and said, "Shall we begin in section six?"

"I'd prefer thirteen," Alphonse answered.

Dressler seemed surprised. "So soon?"

Alphonse nodded. "As I said, we have little time to spare, Doctor. Let's begin with the essential properties and work backwards. I want to make certain that we cover the necessary inventory should I need to cut the inspection short."

"Cut it short?" she asked.

"There is a situation in a nearby system that may require my attention," lied Alphonse. "In the event that I am needed, I would rather have already examined your essential inventory."

"If I might be so bold, Constable, what sort of situation is it?" she asked.

"A classified one," he remarked. "One that I am not at liberty to discuss. However, I will tell you it is a matter of public safety."

She paused. "Terrorism?"

He smiled. "You are astute, Doctor. Very good. I'm afraid I can speak no more of it, though. I'm sure you understand."

"I do, of course," she said, returning his smile. "Please follow me, sir."

I had to say I was pretty impressed with Alphonse's ability to make up stories on the fly. He had a talent for this sort of thing, which was probably why he'd been recruited to be a Constable in the first place.

Dressler led us to an elevator, using her thumbprint to activate it, and pressed the button for the thirteenth floor. I stood there quietly along with Abigail, wondering just what the hell I was thinking when I agreed to come here.

I thumbed the butt of my pistol for no other reason than to double check it was still there. I hated being this close to the Union.

The doors opened and I felt a sweep of cold air brush across my cheeks. It felt ten degrees cooler.

"Right this way, Constable," said Dressler. "You'll find everything the same as your last visit."

We stepped into a cross-shaped hall with a corridor on each side as well as a long hallway directly ahead. It ended with a massive set of double doors twice my size.

I wanted to ask why anyone needed a door this big, but kept my mouth shut.

Doctor Dressler approached a small scanner on the wall and pressed her eye to it. "Identity acknowledged. Please proceed," said the A.I.

The doors opened, sliding apart. What I saw on the other side gave me pause.

It seemed to be a massive storage facility with shelves and crates as far as my eyes could see. There had to be hundreds, maybe thousands, of rows here. A brief glance at the nearest one showed a familiar item casually resting in a small bin—an old Earth-relic, tagged and marked for later reference. It seemed our suspicions had been correct and the Union really was collecting their share of artifacts, probably for decades, if not longer.

If Freddie had been here, I could only imagine his response to all this. Or Hitchens, for that matter. Maybe they could have made sense out of some of these old trinkets, because I certainly couldn't.

But that didn't mean I couldn't steal a few.

"Straight ahead, please," said Dressler, staring at me. I'd apparently been so caught up with my surroundings that I forgot to keep up.

Once I was back in line, the doctor continued forward, leading us to the rear of this massive compartment.

There was no door there, but an opening leading into a small room no larger than the lounge of my ship. It contained nothing but shelves on all sides, with a table in the center.

Dressler walked to the far-right corner. "Verdan," she said.

"Yes, Doctor," said the A.I., her voice coming from above us.

"Open Vault 2771," said Dressler.

I almost asked why anyone needed 2771 vaults, but stopped myself.

"Proceeding," said Verdan.

The shelves in front of Dressler clicked, pulling back into the wall, then moved sideways. How many hidden rooms do we have to get through? I thought as the doctor motioned for us to follow.

Inside, the room was largely empty, surrounded by smooth walls. The only object was a single crate at the center of the floor. It was quite possibly the most pristinely designed space I'd ever seen.

I distrusted it instantly.

Dressler tapped a small screen on the surface of the crate, entering what must have been her authorization code. A light click followed, and she took a step back. "There you are, Constable Malloy."

"Very good," said Alphonse, walking closer to it. As he did, both halves of the lid separated, pulling up and apart.

I felt for my pistol, staying ready for any unexpected crap that might befall us in this underground deathtrap.

Alphonse leaned over the box, eyeing its contents. "It appears the item is intact," he said.

"As you can see, it is still the same as the last inspection," said Dressler. "Shall we move on?"

The Constable paused, looking at me. "I suppose now would be the time."

I glanced at Abigail, who gave me a slight nod, signaling she was ready.

"Yes, well, I'll need to reseal the material," said Dressler. "Please excuse me."

She took a step toward the box.

I took a quick breath. It was now or never.

"That's far enough," I said, pulling my pistol out from inside my jacket. "Back up!"

"E-excuse me?" she said.

"I think you heard him," said Abigail, lifting her own pistol out from under her shirt.

Dressler looked at Alphonse. "Constable?"

"I'm afraid it's a robbery," said Alphonse, frowning. "So sorry, Doctor."

"Hands up," I ordered.

"Th-this is outrageous! Do you have any idea what kind of security measures we have in place around this facility?" asked Dressler.

Abigail grabbed the doctor by her wrist and pulled her close to her waist. "That's why you're coming with us."

"Well, that's not the only reason," said Alphonse. He reached into the box and lifted up a thin green object. It looked like a tube of some kind, sealed on both ends and filled with...something. Alphonse handed it to me.

I examined it closer in my hand. It had a cloudy look to it, like there was smoke inside. "This is it?" I asked.

"Were you expecting something else?" asked Alphonse.

"I don't know," I said, cocking my eye. "Maybe a shiny gem or a giant orb?"

"They have both of those down the hall," he said. "Would you prefer it if we stole those too?"

"Are they worth anything?" I asked.

"If they're in this building, they're worth something. In fact—"

"Hey!" snapped Abigail, tightening her grip on the doctor. "Shouldn't we find a way out of here?"

"Oh, right," I said, stuffing the ancient fuel cell into my leg pocket. "Which way, Doc?"

Dressler squirmed against Abigail uncomfortably. "If you think I'm helping you steal that, you can forget it. Verdan! Initiate security procedure Beta-Gamma-Six-Two-Nine!"

"Proceeding," said Verdan. "Informing Security Forces have been dispatched."

Alphonse's eyes widened. "Oh no."

I godsdamn knew it, I thought.

And here I was, hoping to get out of this place without any trouble.

I pulled my pistol up and cocked the hammer back, aiming it at the doctor's forehead. "You'd better fix what-ever the hell you just did."

Alphonse reached his hand out at Dressler. "Listen to him, please. That man is a trained Renegade. He's not bluffing."

"A Renegade?" she asked. "Constable, what are you doing with this man?"

"I put a bomb in his belly and forced him to follow me," I said, motioning to Alphonse's belly. "If he tries anything, those guts of his will end up all over your clean walls."

"There's a bomb?" she asked, her eyes widening in disbelief as they fell on Alphonse's waist. "You brought a bomb into this facility?!"

Alphonse nodded. "You see the situation now, don't you? I had no choice."

"If you detonate a bomb in here, do you know what kind of chaos you'll unleash? The materials on this level alone are—"

I leaned forward and pressed the barrel into her chest. "Then you'd best do as I say, lady, and help us get out of here."

She furrowed her brow at me. "You had better take that gun out of my face!"

I paused at her tone. She had spunk. I'd give her that much.

"We need to move," said Abigail, shoving the doctor forward. "Those security officers will be here any second."

"She's right," said Alphonse. "Shall we retreat?"

I stared at Dressler, who stared right back at me. "Fine," I said after a short moment. "Try anything else and you're done, Doc."

"I'm no fool," she said. "You're going to kill me no matter what I do."

"Wrong," I countered.

"If you help us, we'll let you go," said Abigail.

"What's it gonna be, Doc?" I asked.

She hesitated to answer. I could see the gears turning in her head as she weighed her options. Help a group of thieves or risk getting killed here and now. "Fine," she said at last. "There's another lift through the main warehouse, back the way we came. It leads to a second security check-point on the surface."

"How about you call off the guards first?" I asked.

"I can't," she said. "Once they've been activated, they have to perform a full check on the identified location."

"We need to hurry," said Alphonse. I was surprised to sense a bit of anxiety in his voice.

I glared at Dressler. "Where to?"

"If you can get to the lift, the security system won't stop you," informed Dressler. "It's on a separate network, used only for emergencies."

"What's the catch?" I asked.

"You'll need my authorization to use it," she said.

"Of course we do," Abigail said.

I crept up next to the doorway, peering through to the previous room with the shelves and into the main ware-house. "Let's head out," I said, motioning for the others to follow. "Everyone, stay behind me. Try not to get yourselves shot."

WE FLED into the warehouse at the exact same moment that the elevator opened. Seven soldiers poured into the atrium, fully armed and ready to stop us.

"Back up!" I barked as soon as I spotted them.

The lead guard shot a burst in my direction, tagging my shield and causing it to flicker. "Shield at 90 percent," said the automated voice inside my ear, a copy of Athena's, although I knew it wasn't her.

I ducked behind the wall, back inside the storage room. "Everyone, stay!" I told them, grabbing Alphonse by the shoulder and slamming him against the shelf beside me. The force knocked an object onto the floor, an old artifact of some sort.

Several more shots came through the opening, keeping me from moving. "They're using suppressing fire to keep us in here," said Alphonse. "I would expect a second group to move in soon."

"No shit, Constable," I muttered, checking my pistol, then raising it beside the doorway. "Abby, stay here and keep these two locked down. I'll be back."

"Is he serious?" asked Dressler, peering up at Alphonse.

"Shut up," said Abigail, still gripping the woman's wrist. "Let the man work." She looked at me, nodding. "Go."

One of the soldiers was moving between two rows in the warehouse, coming toward us. "Be back soon," I muttered, then dashed into the gunfire.

A bullet struck the shield around my leg, lighting me up for a brief second and draining my energy to 80 percent. Not a problem, so long as I was through.

I ran to the nearest soldier, between the two rows of artifacts. I shot him twice in the chest before I was even on him, then collided with his body and slammed him into the nearby shelves. He wheezed when I struck him, and I finished him swiftly with a bullet to the head.

I sprinted from there and slid when I reached a gap between the rows, firing two shots and hitting one of the soldiers in the leg. He screamed, causing the others to return fire, but I was already behind the second row.

I leapt to my feet and continued running. *What I wouldn't give for some grenades right about now.*

I could see the soldiers moving on the other side of the shelves, heading towards me. Immediately, I dropped to the floor and got off a quick couple of shots, hitting two of them in the feet, ripping their boots to shreds and destroying their bones. *That'll slow them down,* I thought.

In a quick scramble, I scurried back up and dashed forward before they had a chance to realize what was going on.

A second later, a spray of gunfire shot up the spot behind me, exactly where I'd been lying, knocking several priceless artifacts to the floor, filling the warehouse with ear-piercing noise.

"He's on the move!" shouted one of the guards. "Head to the rear!"

I reached another gap in the rows and took a hard right, away from the soldiers. I'd have to lose them if I wanted to keep this going.

Can't stay in one place for too long, I thought. *These bastards won't stop until they bleed me dry.*

Before I could enter another row, I heard a gunshot from behind, followed by the flickering light of my shield and the automated voice saying, "Shields at 65 percent."

I reacted with a quick turn, dropping in the process and sliding. I extended my pistol, waiting until I had the pursuing guard in my sights, and then fired.

The bullet struck him in the stomach, and he staggered, but only for a moment. These guys had body armor, enough to protect their abdomen from one or two shots. Before he could react any further, I followed it up with another one, this time at his skull.

He collapsed on his knees, dropping the rifle, and fell forward.

I was already moving, turning back around, toward the room where Abigail and the others were waiting.

Two soldiers came up behind the corpse. "Friendly down!" shouted one of them.

A spray of bullets followed me as I ran.

I took multiple hits, sending my shield into a frenzy, lighting it up so much I thought it might break. "Shield at 30 percent," said the voice in my ear.

I reached the end of the row where the first soldier was

lying dead, then turned to see Abigail and Alphonse watching me from inside the room.

There were still soldiers in the open area of the warehouse, and they didn't hesitate to fire when I burst through the rows.

I ran to the room, firing blindly at the guards, less concerned with hitting them than just getting out. "Shield at 10 percent," said the voice.

"Your turn!" I snapped as I reached the room, barely getting inside before my shield gave out.

Several bullets struck the wall to our right, across from the open doorway.

Abigail took Dressler by the hand and pushed her behind Alphonse. "Stay," she ordered, then looked at me. "Watch them while I handle the rest!"

I was on the floor, back against the wall in a reverse-prone position. "You got it," I said, wheezing from all the running.

Abigail burst into the bullet storm, instantly taking fire. Her shield lit up, but she was already shooting, popping one soldier in his chest before he had a chance to understand what was going on.

The two men who'd been chasing me arrived from between the rows, charging at her. They fired as they came, managing to get two shots on her shield before she retaliated.

With the pistol in her hand, she reached for her electric baton, activated the charge, and stabbed one of the men in the stomach. He fell to the floor and spasmed like he was having a seizure.

She extended the baton, brought it up above her head, and slammed it across the second guard's neck.

I heard the crack from all the way inside the room, where I was watching. "Ouch," I muttered with a cringe.

In only a few seconds, both men had been incapacitated.

Abigail turned her attention to the only remaining soldier. He fired his rifle, sniping her shield—first in the stomach, then in the shoulder.

Abigail lifted her pistol, began marching towards him, and squeezed the trigger.

I heard two shots, out of view, followed by the sound of a body hitting the floor.

The nun returned a second later, casually reentering the room. "Everyone ready?"

"Y-you killed all those men?" muttered Dr. Dressler. "How is...how is that even possible?"

Alphonse motioned with his hand toward the warehouse. "I hope you understand the severity of your situation, Doctor. Now please show us the way so that we can leave you in peace."

"You heard the man," I said. "Al doesn't want to die today."

"Death does not agree with me," he added.

"Dispatching additional personnel," informed the A.I. over the loudspeakers.

Abigail grabbed Dressler by the wrist. "Let's go!"

We fled along the nearby wall, passing by several of the formerly living guards. I was in the lead, with Alphonse, Dr. Dressler, and Abigail right behind me. This wasn't the way I had hoped for today to go, but it certainly could have gone much worse.

When we reached the edge of the warehouse, Dressler pointed. "Through the second door!"

I glanced over my shoulder. "If we walk in there and an alarm goes off, so help me..."

"It's safe, I promise," she insisted, running up beside me and letting the scanner examine her eye. It beeped and the door slid open, showing a dimly lit corridor. "Through here, then a left, and it's straight until you reach the—"

"Contact front!" shouted someone from the other end of the warehouse.

The soldiers fired, causing us to rush inside and forego the discussion. I yanked the doctor into the hall, both of us falling on our faces. Abigail pushed Alphonse ahead of her, taking a shot in the back so he didn't have to.

The door closed behind her, and we hurried to our feet. "Run!" Abigail snapped. "We need to go!"

I dragged Dressler behind me as we moved. The lights overhead began to come on, one at a time, further into the hall. We ran faster than they could activate, rounding the corner and reaching the far end in under thirty seconds.

I heard voices coming from the previous direction

Someone was shouting orders. "Get this godsdamn door open!"

Dressler ran up to the elevator doors, which were only a few more paces away. She then tapped a code into the touch pad, allowing us to pile inside.

"That was almost bad," I said, once we were in.

A loud, shattering sound came from down the hall, and I heard footsteps clapping, growing louder.

As the doors closed, shadows emerged from around the corner, followed by men with guns, clad in Union armor.

"There!" shouted the closest one.

I waved right as the doors shut, the second before they opened fire, denting the elevator metal.

Dr. Dressler nearly fell back into Alphonse's arms, scared to death.

I looked at her, then at Alphonse, and gave him an obvious smirk. "Save it for later, Al," I said, turning forward and cracking my neck. "We might have more killin' left to do."

8

THE DOORS OPENED behind three men in lab coats. Before they could even turn around, Abigail had a pistol on one and the end of her baton on another. "Don't move."

"W-what is this? Who are—"

"Keep quiet!" she snapped, nudging the man with the barrel.

"After you," I said to Dressler.

The doctor stepped through the lift doors and into what I guessed was a laboratory. "Everyone, please, just do as they say," Dressler said.

"Where are we?" asked Abigail, still with both her weapons against the two doctors.

"F-first floor, laboratory twelve," said one of them.

Abigail lowered the pistol, but only to her hip. The

barrel remained pointed. "Which way to reach the courtyard?"

The man bent to his right and pointed.

I tapped Abigail's shoulder and motioned for her to step back, along with Alphonse and Dressler. With everyone out of the way, I asked if there was anyone else in this lab.

"Only us," said the second doctor.

"In you go," I said, nodding at the elevator, and they did exactly what I told them. "Press the button for the bottom floor and don't come back here for an hour."

They each nodded, fear all over their faces.

We waited for the doors to close and the elevator to descend, just to be sure.

Abigail dragged Dressler behind her, heading in the direction the other doctor had suggested. "Time to go!"

I nodded at Alphonse, and we both followed.

After a short corridor, we found a set of double doors, which opened into a field of finely cut grass. This must have been the side entrance. It was secured with a scanner, so you couldn't leave without authorization, and there didn't seem to be any handles or devices on the other side. That meant that once we were outside, there would be no going back.

If we ended up in the middle of a firefight, it would also mean little to no cover.

Nowhere to run but forward.

"Are we ready?" I asked each of my fellow fugitives.

"I could stand to stay behind," said Dressler. "Please, you don't need me anymore, do you?"

"Nice try," said Abigail.

The doctor swallowed. "I can't believe this is happening."

I fled through the door, the others right behind me, my pistol at the ready. A sudden breeze flew across my cheeks and, for a moment, it was nice, like being in a glade near a brook, the total opposite of where I actually was. It was almost like I wasn't robbing the Union and trying to escape with two hostages at my side and one of the galaxy's most powerful artifacts in my godsdamn pocket.

I could see the entrance to the landing platform straight ahead of us, across the field. It was a wide area with thin towers on all sides, which could have been anything from overhead lights to turrets, for all I knew. I cursed myself for not scouting this location more before coming down, but there hadn't been enough time, not with General Brigham tracking us, although I certainly couldn't confirm that he was. I'd been too shortsighted, rushing onto this asshole of a planet. Oh well. It wouldn't be the first time I'd played fast and—

"Stop them! They're heading to that ship!" shouted a husky voice to my left.

A group of armed guards filed out of the front of the building. A quick glance revealed it was the same squad that had escorted us into the building after we'd landed.

"Run!" I shouted, taking Dressler's hand and pulling her into the open grass.

Several shots fired on my position. Dressler screamed, surprising me with how loud her voice could get. For such an angry-looking woman, she sure could project herself.

"Wait! They have a hostage!" shouted one of the soldiers.

"Doesn't matter! Keep firing!" returned another.

"W-what did he just say?!" asked Dressler.

"Keep up!" snapped Alphonse.

I let go of the doctor and pulled out my pistol, ready to return fire. I got off a couple of shots, hitting the windows behind the soldiers and forcing them to take cover. That would buy us a few moments.

I came to a quick stop, dragging my heel in the grass and turning around. In seconds, I was facing the soldiers, my arm steady with the gun.

Right as Abigail was about to pass beside me, I raised my other hand and motioned at her to toss me her gun. She tossed it at me and I caught it, wrapping my fingers around the butt as I brought it around toward the other men, along with my own weapon.

Using both pistols, I unloaded a steady flow of bullets, making sure the men stayed down. There were only four soldiers, from what I could see, which meant the others were somewhere else. There had been six originally when they'd met us at the loading dock.

I began to back up, continuing to fire in a steady

rhythm. These guns each carried two dozen bullets, and I only had one spare magazine. If we didn't get out of here soon, things might not end so well.

"Jace!" shouted Abigail, the urgency in her voice telling me it was time to go. I turned around, replacing my backwards jog with a hard, forward run.

I saw the two remaining soldiers near the *Star*, holding rifles and waiting for our group.

They looked like they were about to fire on Dressler, when I managed to get a shot off, hitting my own ship. This forced them to hit the ground. One of them shouted something to the other, which caused them both to aim at me. Apparently, they viewed me as the larger threat.

That was a mistake.

Abigail pushed Dressler into Alphonse's arms. The Constable caught the doctor and brought her to the ground with him, while Abigail continued forward.

The nun leapt into the air, taking out her baton and activating it. The pole extended, a spark igniting at the end. In a hard swipe, she brought the object down, hitting the first soldier square in the face, breaking his nose and spattering blood into the air.

The second man raised his weapon, ready to shoot her before she could get any closer.

I squeezed the trigger on both guns, but I'd finally run out.

The soldier stood there with Abigail in his sights. She

wasn't reacting, which made me think her shield must be depleted.

I reached for the last remaining magazine, hoping I still had enough time to get a shot off before that soldier did what he was about to—

Alphonse ran straight into him, knocking the gun to the side, right as the soldier fired. The man turned on him, but Alphonse responded with a kick to his stomach, then a quick tap to the man's throat. The soldier fell on his knees, gasping for air, like his windpipe had collapsed. Alphonse took his head in his arms and twisted, snapping the man's neck before he even knew what was happening to him.

Abigail was gawking at what the Constable had just done. "What did you—"

"I suggest we depart," said Alphonse, motioning to the ship. "More of them will be here soon."

I ran over to Dressler and helped her up, then joined the others. "Nice one, Al," I said as I passed him.

He nodded. "Happy to help, Captain."

Another burst of gunfire followed, hitting the ship as we ran into the lift. "Siggy, close the godsdamn hatch!" I shouted.

"Right away, sir," answered the A.I.

The lift raised as multiple shots ricocheted through the shrinking opening. "Take cover!" I ordered.

Everyone ducked as the bullets bounced overhead, hitting metal and disappearing into the walls.

"Get us in the air, Siggy!" I shouted just as the door closed.

"As you wish, sir," he said. "Activating thrusters."

I crawled my way to the stairs but stayed down, knowing better than to move too much or risk a deflecting bullet.

The gunfire continued as we lifted into the air. We all stayed on our faces, waiting for the bulletstorm to be replaced by the silence of space.

The engines activated, rumbling through the entire ship before the stabilizers had a chance to kick in. As it settled, I felt us lift off the ground.

"Everyone okay?" I asked now that we were rocketing away from the planet.

"I think so," said Abigail, who was on her knees.

"Constable…are you all right?" asked Dr. Dressler, still out of breath. She edged her way closer to Alphonse, who was lying on his back. "Y-you're bleeding!"

Alphonse tried to stand but stopped and clutched his stomach. When he took his palm away, I could finally see the blood.

I sat forward, pushing myself up from the stairs. "Alphonse?" I said, trying to get a better look. He had sweat all over his forehead, strain in his eyes. Something was definitely wrong.

Abigail ran over to him and pushed the kid on his back. "Lie down for a second and let me see," she ordered, lifting his shirt above his stomach.

"I'm sorry," he muttered. His eyes fluttered, like he was about to pass out. "I…should have been faster…"

"Idiot!" snapped Abigail. "Why didn't you run faster?" She looked at me, her eyes fixed with anger. "Get me the godsdamn med kit!"

9

By the time I returned with the med kit, Alphonse had lost consciousness. Abigail managed to get the wound wrapped, but without the necessary tools, we wouldn't be able to excise the bullet.

I had to leave him with Abigail and Dressler while I made my way to the cockpit. I didn't want to, but someone had to man the cannons and fly us out of there, and I couldn't rely on Siggy to do everything. Impressive as he was, Sigmond could only handle so many things at once.

I entered a command on the console and took the control sticks, leading us away from the planet. Before I could even call down to check on Abigail or bring up the camera feed from the cargo bay, Siggy informed me that we had a tail.

By the look of it, three of them. All Union strike ships.

"Out of the fire…" I muttered. "Siggy! How long before *Titan* comes out of that tunnel?"

"Approximately eight minutes, sir," he answered.

"Close enough! Let's see if we can make it there before those ships catch up to us."

"Based on their current rate of acceleration, I do not believe that will be possible," informed Siggy.

I cursed, then activated the holo display to show the system we were in. I looked frantically for somewhere to go, anything with a narrow enough space to—

I paused on the fourth planet in the system, the closest to Priscilla. It had a thin but wide ring of rocks around it, like many other class-3 planets. A quick analysis revealed that this world also had a whopping seventy-six moons.

"Siggy, I'm taking us behind that ring, close to the planet. Make sure we don't hit anything," I ordered.

"Acknowledged, sir," said the A.I.

If I could buy some time before *Titan* arrived, I might be able to get away without any excessive damage, but I'd have to stay out of their line-of-sight. I hated not being able to take them all head-on, but I couldn't risk my crew or my ship, not if there was a better way out.

I brought the *Renegade Star* within orbit of the ringed planet then reduced our speed to a slow crawl as we neared the ring itself—a thin spread of ice and rock, twice the size of the planet.

"Time to lay the traps," I said, sweeping my finger across the console, dropping one of the mines that Athena had given me. "Let's see if these things are as good as she said."

I placed six mines, nearly all of them—three below the ring and three above—and brought my ship to the rear of it, nearer to the planet.

I watched the holo as it showed all three ships drawing closer to my position. The centermost strike ship had its shield raised, encompassing all of them. I activated my own, waiting for them.

Any second now, I thought.

The ships neared the ring, heading above and ignoring the bottom.

I backed up closer to the planet.

The three ships moved together, their shield grazing the ring and causing the particles and fragments to swirl and displace.

The first of the three mines reacted, its sensors detecting the incoming vessels, and it homed itself towards them. The mine ignited right as it reached the shield, exploding in a mess of blue plasma, lighting up the darkness for a brief second and causing the protective layer to fracture and flicker, like it was about to break. My mouth fell open at the sight. Talk about a bomb! My old mines didn't hold a candle to these. "That's what I'm talking about!" I shouted, smacking my console.

The ship closest to the ring jerked slightly as the shield settled.

I dropped the *Renegade Star* further below the ring,

priming my quad cannons as I tracked the ships' movements.

The second mine reacted as they drew closer to the end of the ring, and it lunged itself towards them, exploding at the same distance as the first. The shield surrounding the ships flickered once again as the blue light encapsulated it. The shield cracked and broke, finally dissolving as the damage became too great for it to bear.

The three ships separated, moving away now that the shield was gone. Since they had no reason to stick together, they could move freely. It was hard to say if things had just improved or gotten worse for me.

Or for them.

I tracked each of the ships, all of them moving in different directions. The first continued along the same path, headed unknowingly toward the next mine, while the second and third broke apart and headed to each side of the ring, no doubt to flank me.

I'd be ready for all of them. I clutched my control stick and began firing a spray into the ring, targeting the nearest of the two that were breaking free. My shots went straight through the ice, obliterating rocks and creating clouds of heavy dust as I continued firing at the moving ship. As it neared the edge of the ring, one of my torpedoes struck it in the side, grazing its secondary engine. The ship spun repeatedly, out of control, going directly into the particles of the ring and displacing them further.

This was my chance.

With another spread, I fired at the ship, missing all but two blasts, which hit the vessel at its center, clear through the cockpit, breaking the ship apart.

An explosion boomed from further down the ring as the first pilot inadvertently triggered the third mine. He was gone instantly, which left only one to contend with.

I charged forward, right as the last ship came around the other side of the ring. We fired our cannons together at one another.

I missed most of the spread, while his struck my shield. The cockpit shook violently, and I held on to my seat while the stabilizers adjusted. If not for my shield, it would have been far worse.

"Sir, the slip tunnel is opening," informed Siggy.

"Not now!" I barked, holding the control sticks and trying to target the other vessel. He rolled sideways, out of my spread. "Fuck!"

This ship moved better than the others, adjusting for my actions. This guy was a pro, I acknowledged, but he wouldn't beat me here. Not after I'd gone through all the trouble of stealing that core.

I targeted the nearest mine, one of the three resting beneath the ring, none of which had been detonated yet, and fired.

The mine triggered, exploding in a wild display. It was too far to actually hit the other ship, but for a moment, he stopped firing, probably surprised.

The strike ship wavered, and I fired off his right side,

forcing him further toward the other mines. When he was close enough, I shot again, but this time, I hit the second bomb, and it lit the ring up, catching the ship with it.

The enemy vessel tumbled, half of its left side gone. Before it could do anything else, I unloaded a string of torpedoes into him, landing two direct hits. He was gone in seconds, turned to dust and scraps.

"Captain Hughes," came a voice from out of nowhere. I recognized it as Athena's.

"I'm here," I answered, trying to pull myself out of my focus. My whole body had been tense without me even realizing it. I tried to relax, taking a long breath and exhaling.

"This is *Titan*. Prepare for departure, please. We must leave quickly."

"Right, I'm coming back now. Hold your position," I answered, turning the *Renegade Star* towards the recently opened slip tunnel and the giant moon that had just left it.

My thrusters kicked in and the ship began to move, headed straight for *Titan*. "Siggy, take us close enough for the tractor beam to grab us. Let me know when we're there," I said.

"Understood, sir," said Sigmond.

I watched as my holo changed to a close up of *Titan*, with our new coordinates locked in.

With a quick breath, I steadied my calm and unlocked my harness, pulling it over my head. I got up and headed to the door, intent on checking back with Abigail and the others. I'd left them in the cargo bay, hoping they could handle the situation themselves, but Abby wasn't a medic or a surgeon. She couldn't save a dying man, not if it came to that. Taking life came easy to me and her, but saving it... that took another kind of skill, and it was beyond us.

I jogged through the ship, passing through the lounge and into the rear corridor. When I finally reached the cargo bay, I found Abby resting on her knees with Alphonse's head in her lap. His eyes were closed and I instantly thought the worst.

But no, I immediately noticed, his chest was rising. He was only asleep. The nun had managed, somehow, to keep him alive through all the fighting, through all the death and killing taking place beyond these walls. Somehow, this little prick was hanging on.

And, much to my own surprise, I was glad for it.

10

THE SECOND WE docked on *Titan*, Athena asked me to head to the elevator. I'd have to get the core to Engineering…and fast.

I didn't waste any time.

The *Star's* engines were still settling when I bolted out of my ship's cargo bay and into the megastructure, leaving Abigail to tend to the injured Constable and the no-doubt confused Dr. Dressler beside him.

I saw the elevator doors open before I even reached them. Racing through the corridor towards them, I was surprised to see someone already inside. It was Athena, standing tall and vibrant, with Lex beside her, smiling. "Mr. Hughes!" called the little girl, waving at me.

I slowed, stopping when I reached the lift. "What's this

about?" I asked, looking at Athena. "Why isn't Lex with Octavia or Freddie?"

"I've asked Lex to assist us in this process," explained Athena.

"Assist?" I asked.

She stepped aside, inviting me to enter. "Please," she said, gesturing with her hand. "I'll explain on the way. We must hurry."

I decided to trust her and boarded the elevator. As the doors closed, I felt Lex's hand touch my sleeve. I glanced down and saw her smiling at me. I couldn't help but return it. "You okay, kid?"

She nodded. "Did you have fun on your trip?"

"Always do," I said, leaving out the part where I almost took a bullet in the face.

"I had fun too," said Lex enthusiastically.

"Oh yeah?" I asked.

She grinned. "Me and Camilla played while you were gone. Athena helped too!"

I glanced up at the Cognitive. "That right?"

"The children found their way into one of the lower sections of the ship. I escorted them out," explained Athena.

The elevator slowed as we reached our destination. "You still haven't said where we're taking the core," I said right as the lift opened. The deck looked dark and dimly lit, from what I could see, like all the life in this place had been drained out.

Lex and I stepped out of the lift, while Athena remained inside. I looked back when I realized she wasn't with us. "You coming?" I asked.

"You will require the child's dermal implants in order to gain entry to the engine room," said Athena. "The emitters on this level are currently inoperable, due to the power shortage we are experiencing. It seems I used too much during our stay in the slip tunnel. I'll regain control once you insert the core."

"You're not making this easy," I said, but didn't bother asking any questions. If *Titan* was losing so much power that Athena couldn't even display herself in certain areas of the ship, we probably didn't have much time before the entire megastructure ran out of juice. I took Lex by the hand. "Ready to do this, kid?"

She nodded. "Ready!"

We left Athena and began moving to the far end of this part of the deck. There were seats and consoles sitting everywhere, giving the appearance of a bustling facility where one might expect to see dozens of personnel, only now it was totally empty. I felt like I was running through an abandoned ship, which I supposed was exactly true, since it had been nearly two thousand years since living humans walked these halls.

Lex and I came upon a gray door, taller than me and three times as wide. It had no handles or nearby pads to enter any codes. Nothing to tell me what to do next. I stood there for a second, stupidly ignorant of how to proceed.

The little girl beside me released my hand and approached the door. I opened my mouth to tell her to wait, when suddenly, a soft blue light emitted from above our heads. It was a scanner, resting on top of the door, shining down on us. I blinked, watching it curiously before I realized what it must be picking up.

I glanced back down at Lex to see her tattoos lighting up, the same way they had every time she'd played with an artifact. She glowed in the dark, illuminating the area around us.

Lex raised her hand to the door, and suddenly, it opened, cracking apart with a heavy grind.

"Nice one, kid," I muttered, staring at the opening doors.

"Told you I could help," she said.

I smiled, nodding. "That you did, kid."

We continued forward, running further into the deeper recesses of Engineering. More empty consoles and seats on each side. I was surprised to find Lex unfazed by this, as so many children seemed to fear dark places. Instead, she was curious enough to explore, to keep going farther.

And so we did, running straight through the final corridor to reach the engine room.

As we arrived, we found the ceiling had opened up, fading into darkness as it stretched high into the ship. Lights blinked on the nearby dash, close to a massive tube, which I assumed must be the engine. It was difficult to know if this was the place or if the core itself was elsewhere, but given the way the tube had been placed—center of the room, surrounded by consoles and lights—I assumed it must be.

Lex began to glow again, only this time, she didn't have to touch anything. Instead, something on the console reacted. I stepped closer to see a slit open, round and about the size of the core itself.

I reached into my pocket, pulling out the power source. "All that work, just for this," I muttered, staring at the core. I brought it above the console. "This better work, Athena."

I slid the container inside, finding a perfect fit. There was a hard click, followed by a humming sound. The machine twisted the core where it sat, rotating it to the left, nearly all the way, then slightly to the right. I waited, my eyes lingering once it stopped. "That's it?" I asked. "Is it broken or—"

The console sucked the core inside itself, startling me, and the humming noise grew louder, vibrating the floor beneath our feet. "What's that?" asked Lex.

I grabbed her hand to keep her steady, taking the nearby wall with my other. A burst of green light boomed from inside the tube, illuminating the surrounding area as the glow spread into the upper recesses of the ship, high above our heads and into the vertical tunnel. Another burst quickly followed, and then another. Rapid firing continued while the lights began to blur into one another, until the bursts became a steady stream of glowing light.

The tunnel above us stretched so far into the ship that I couldn't see the end.

Lex and I stood together, lost in the array of color. If Athena was to be believed, this was one of the most powerful engines in the galaxy, and now it was coming online.

The vibrating floor and the sounds of the core began to slow, like a storm was ending. After a few more moments, the chaos seemed to settle, replaced with the electric hum of an idling engine.

The overhead lights turned on at once, surprising us both. It happened one at a time, with sections of the deck lighting up, bit by bit, until everything was normal. The consoles powered on next, blinking red and yellow dots filling the workstations with activity, despite having no one there to operate them. This formerly dead part of the ship suddenly felt very much alive.

Through all this, the core never lost its powerful green glow, however, and it continued to dominate the room, drawing my eyes like I was a bug.

Athena popped into existence, right in front of us. "Well done," she said at last.

I was glad to see her emitters back online, the final sign I needed to know the core had worked.

Lex ran up to her. "Did we do it right?"

"Yes, you did, Lex," said the Cognitive. "Excellent work."

Lex cheered, turning to me, like I was expected to join in. I conceded a smile, and she seemed to think that was good enough.

"What's the plan, Athena? What do we do now?" I asked, staring up into the bowels of the core above my head. The lights went deep into the megastructure, and I couldn't help but be taken aback by it.

"Now?" asked Athena, stepping closer to me, a concerned look in her eyes. "Now, Captain Hughes, I believe it is time for us to run."

"*TITAN's ENERGY* reserves had nearly been depleted when we arrived," explained Athena.

We were back in slipspace, headed as far away from the godsdamn Union as we could get. I stood on the bridge, along with Abigail and Freddie, who'd rushed to meet me here so we could formulate some kind of strategy.

Abigail continued. "We had enough to open a final tunnel, should we have needed it. Thankfully, the mission had been a success, and Captain Hughes managed to get the core back in time."

"Lucky," said Freddie.

"Not for Alphonse," I said. "Speaking of, how's he doing?"

Abigail shook her head. "Critical. He needs surgery. Octavia is handling it, although I'm uncertain whether she has the necessary tools or experience."

"She's a former medic," said Freddie.

"Hardly the same as a surgeon," argued Abigail.

"Please, everyone," interjected Athena. "Soon *Titan's* systems will be back online. That includes more than the engines."

"What are you saying?" asked Abby.

"This vessel contains a medical bay with multiple regeneration pods. Once the core has fully rebooted and all systems have been restored, all serious injuries can be seen to."

"What's all that now?" I asked. "Are you saying you can heal Alphonse?"

"Certainly," said the Cognitive, like it was obvious. "*Titan* was built with the most sophisticated medical equipment available. In addition to the regeneration pods, we also have a complete line of surgical units."

"Jace, we have to get Alphonse to one of those pods," said Abigail.

"We can't," said Freddie. "The systems haven't come back yet."

"Correct," said Athena. "It will be some time before all areas of *Titan* are restored, including the medical bay."

"Athena, can you show us the feed of Octavia and Alphonse?" I asked.

She nodded then waved her hand, changing the wall behind her to screen to show the landing bay, near the *Renegade Star*.

"Hey, you didn't freeze up this time," observed Freddie.

"A result of the new core," she explained.

"It's nice to see something has improved," I remarked.

Octavia was in her chair, sitting beside an unconscious Alphonse, with Hitchens and Bolin on the other side of him. The two men were handing her equipment, helping with what I could only guess was some sort of surgery.

"Can you open a channel?" I asked.

Athena nodded. "Speak when ready, Captain."

Octavia currently had a metal object inside of Alphonse's chest, so I waited a moment before I spoke. When she brought the tool away from him and there was no danger in accidentally nicking an artery, I said, "Can anyone hear me?"

Octavia flinched at the sound of my voice. "Captain?" she said.

"Yeah, Athena patched me through. How's Alphonse? Did you get the bullet out?" I asked.

She relaxed. "Not yet," she said, shaking her head. "We're still working on it. I think I'll have it out of him soon, but I'm concerned about internal bleeding should we remove it. The bullet is in a delicate position."

"Is it possible to keep it contained?" asked Abigail.

"He's stable for the moment, but I can't promise he won't bleed out if we leave him this way," said Octavia.

"Athena says she has a way to fix him, but it'll take time," I said.

Octavia looked at Hitchens. "Fix him?" She glanced back at the ceiling. "How?"

"There's a medical bay on the ship, but power's still

being restored. We need you to keep him alive for—" I glanced at Athena. "How long?"

"Enough power should be restored in thirty minutes, approximately," said the Cognitive. "However, this is only an estimate. The process has not been attempted in quite some time."

"Right, we'll take our chances," I said. "Did you get all that, Octavia?"

"I did," she said, wiping some blood from Alphonse's chest. "I'll do what I can until you're ready."

"Right," I said, motioning with my hand to Athena. "That's all for now."

The screen went dark.

"Things are looking up," said Freddie. "If the medical bay is operational, of course."

I nodded. "It will be, I'm sure."

"You sound positive about that," said Abigail.

I shrugged. I honestly didn't know what to expect, but we wouldn't know anything until Athena brought that department back online. Until then, it was better to hope for the best.

If the plan fell apart, Octavia would have to step up and do the surgery, for better or worse. Those were really the only two options. Either the medical pod saved the Constable…or Octavia did. Either way, there wasn't much I could do about it, and I hated worrying about things I had no say in.

Better to focus on what I *could* control. "We need to do

something about that woman too," I said, changing the subject.

"What woman?" asked Freddie.

"Dressler," said Abigail. "We brought her back from Priscilla."

"You did *what*?!" asked Freddie. "When were you going to mention that?"

"When we had time," said the nun.

"She's in Abby's old room on the *Star*," I explained. "I'll go check on her. She's probably freaking out."

"You've been back for a few hours now. Has she been there this whole time?" asked Freddie.

I shrugged and got to my feet. "She's fine."

"Captain, before you leave," said Athena. She teleported beside me, causing me to stop abruptly. "Due to our creating this slip tunnel, we are being forced to use our energy in such a way that *Titan*'s restoration will take longer than normal. If we stop for only an hour, we can have all major systems back online, including the medical facility as well as weapons and shields."

"Weapons?" I asked. "Lady, why didn't you say so? Pull out of this pipe as soon as you can."

"Captain, are you sure about that?" asked Freddie.

"What's not to be sure of?" asked Abigail. "Alphonse's life is on the line."

I raised my brow. "Since when do you care about the Constable? I thought you hated that guy."

"I don't hate him," she snapped with a harsher tone

than I expected. "He just... he saved me down there. I don't want him to die because of it."

"So you feel like you owe him something. Is that it?" I asked. "It's your guilt that's making you care?"

"No, it's not that," she said, pausing. "Or maybe it is. I don't know. I just don't want him to die."

I walked closer to her, until I was less than a meter away. "I don't want him to die either. Gods know why." I laughed, shaking my head. "But don't forget where you are."

She scoffed. "And where is that?"

"In the middle of a war," I answered.

11

"WHAT EXACTLY DO you plan on doing with me, sir?" asked Doctor Dressler. The woman scowled at me with accusatory eyes. It was the kind of look I used to get all the time, back when I was a kid. Always the vagrant, always the suspect. In this case, I actually was the one responsible, but she wasn't going to get the satisfaction of hearing me say it. Sure, I had just kidnapped this woman and brought her to my ship against her will, but that was beside the point.

"Listen, lady," I said, never one to apologize. "I don't know if you realize it or not, but your own people were down there trying to kill you. They shot at all of us, not just me. Not just Abigail. All of us."

"That's because what you stole is more valuable than a single life, including mine," she said.

"Is that a fact?" I asked, leaning against the door panel

with my arms crossed. Unlike Alphonse, who was a trained assassin and spy, I decided not to keep my gun pointed at her face the entire time we talked. That didn't mean I still wouldn't keep my distance. There was always a chance she was more than she appeared. Abigail had taught me that. "The Union doesn't give a damn about you, lady. They don't give a damn about anybody. Doesn't matter who you are or what your job is." I started to laugh. "For gods' sake, you were the lead scientist in one of their most prestigious facilities in the entire galaxy, and they *still* almost killed you. The way I see it, you don't owe the Union anything, especially loyalty."

"Are you seriously giving me a lecture on ethics and loyalty right now?" she asked. "That's interesting, coming from a Renegade. Don't you people murder and steal on a daily basis?"

"Well, I do try," I said, giving her a wink.

She scowled at me again, apparently not liking my charming personality. Her loss. "Just let me go and I promise not to tell anyone anything," she said.

"I'll tell you what, Doc," I began. "Have a little patience and sit your ass in this room for just a bit longer, give me a chance to get my crap in order, then, when I have a spare second, I'll give you a shuttle and send you on your merry way. How's that?"

She stared at me for a moment, an odd look in her eyes, like she was waiting for me to take it back. "Is this some kind of joke?" she asked.

"No joke," I told her, speaking only the truth. "I wouldn't lie about letting you go. Despite what you may think of me, I ain't the bad guy here. Not this time, contrary to how much I might want to be."

"Why would you just let me go like that?" she asked.

"Because it's one less mouth to feed. One less person to take care of," I explained. "And honestly, lady, you just ain't worth the trouble. I got a crew to look after, but that doesn't include you."

"Good," she answered, not hiding her annoyance with me. "How long before I can leave?"

I chuckled at her blunt attitude. "Gimme a few days. You can go after we put some distance between the Union and this ship. Fair enough?"

"You kidnapped me and you're asking if this is fair?" she asked.

"Right," I said, tapping my chin. "Well, it'll have to do."

I shut the door between us, leaving her in the room to marinate on our talk. She'd probably call me a monster in her head, tell herself I was nothing but a dog, and she'd be right.

I'd always been an animal.

I received a message from Athena on my way to the

landing bay. "We will emerge from slipspace momentarily, Captain."

"How long until you have the med bay up and running?" I asked, making my way through the corridor.

"Not long. I suggest you begin transporting the patient immediately," her disembodied voice told me.

I started jogging, winding through the hall and nearing the final turn before the landing bay. The second I entered, I spotted Octavia next to Alphonse, with Bolin and Hitchens wiping their hands. They appeared to have blood on them. "Hey!" I shouted. "How's he looking?"

"Still alive," Octavia told me.

"What's with the blood?" I asked as I approached, nodding to the two burly men a few meters from Octavia.

"I couldn't use my hands to do everything, and it got a little messier than I anticipated," she explained. "I was concerned that if we didn't act soon—"

"Did it work?" I asked.

She nodded. "As well as to be expected."

I stood over the Constable, watching him breathe. I guess you could've called him asleep, but he didn't look like it. There was a peacefulness to sleep, something he didn't have right now. With sweat on his cheeks and blood on his chest, soaking his shirt, the poor bastard looked like a mess.

"We need to move him," I said.

"Where?" asked Octavia.

I motioned at Bolin. "Think you can help carry him?" I asked.

Bolin set the cloth down and, along with Hitchens, came back over to the Constable's table. "I'll help however I can."

"Me too," said Hitchens.

I nodded, looking at Octavia again. "We're taking him to the medical bay, the place I told you about with the pods. Athena says they'll be online soon, so we need to hurry."

"That's good news, but how do you expect to transport him?" she asked.

"Wait here," I said, then took off toward the *Renegade Star*'s loading deck.

I returned a few minutes later with my hover cart, bringing it just beside Alphonse. "You want to take him on *that*?" asked Octavia.

"Why not?" I asked.

She sighed. "I guess it's fine. Just be careful with him. Too much movement could upset the wound. Doctor Hitchens, would you mind assisting the captain?"

"Of course," said Hitchens. He walked next to Alphonse's feet, placing his hands on the Constable's ankles and giving me a short nod.

I waited for Octavia to move, then got in close beside Alphonse's right side, near his midsection, with Bolin across from me. Together, along with Hitchens, we lifted Alphonse off the table and moved him gently onto the hover cart.

"Be extremely careful," cautioned Octavia, rolling further out of the way, once we had the Constable secured. "The slightest bump could dislodge that bullet. If that happens, there won't be anything I, or anyone, can do."

"We'll be careful. Come on, Bolin. You're coming too. All three of you are." I started to move the cart, walking hurriedly but carefully toward the exit corridor. "Let's go save this kid's life."

WE DISEMBARKED from the elevator on deck 19, not far from the medical bay. Athena directed me as we went, suggesting that it would still be several minutes before the facilities were back online.

We'd just arrived out of the slip tunnel, which meant *Titan*'s systems could finally power on. It was just going to take some time, that's all.

I led the group to the third hall, which we took to the seventh room. It was clear this was the right place, because it was open and didn't have a door attached, making for easy access. I imagined that whoever built this place must have wanted passengers to be able to come and go as they pleased.

We pulled the cart inside the med bay, minding the archway so as not to bump the patient and accidentally kill him.

I stopped, turning around to examine the room, and found myself surprised by all the machines. There were large pods all along the walls, ten on each side, with an enclosed room in the center-back, which appeared to have a closed door and glass windows. From a glance, I could see shelves of medical supplies inside.

"Athena, what's next?" I asked the empty room, glancing at the ceiling.

"Power is being restored to this deck. Please place the subject in the surgical pod," answered the Cognitive.

"Which one?" asked Octavia.

"A moment, please," said Athena.

I heard a small beep to my left. One of the pods lit up, its lid raising to reveal a cushioned interior. "That's our sign," I said.

"Proceed when ready," said Athena.

Bolin and I lifted Alphonse out of the cart and gently placed him inside the pod. He groaned when he was seated, and for a second, I thought he might wake up. Instead, his head flopped down against his shoulder and he let out a wheeze. Bolin took the kid's chin and moved it so his head was facing straight, then we backed away.

The pod door closed immediately, and the entire machine tilted and moved, positioning Alphonse so he was on his back.

We watched as the pod filled with a gentle light. I got in close, as did the others. Several small sticks—no, they were claws, extended from within the pod, each one glowing. One of them drew closer to Alphonse's chest, hovering momentarily before it finally dove inside of him, phasing through to where the bullet waited.

"It must be hard light," said Octavia.

"Hard light?" asked Bolin.

"The same thing Athena is made of," she responded.

"Fascinating," muttered Hitchens.

I watched as several more claws joined the first, and after a moment, they began to retract, bringing the metal slug with them. It popped free of the hole, sliding out with ease.

Some blood followed, but not as much as I expected. The claws responded by transforming into a syringe. It moved to the side of the pod and withdrew a gel-like substance, which it then proceeded to eject into the wound, filling it.

The blood stopped soon enough, and the claws fully retracted, disappearing completely.

I was about to ask if that was all there was to it, when a small tube popped out from behind Alphonse's neck. It extended itself directly into his skin. The tube filled with liquid, going into his body.

"The object has been successfully removed and the subject's tissue will regrow within the hour," said Athena, her voice coming from overhead. "Vitals are holding."

I heard Hitchens breathe a sigh of relief next to me. I turned to see him lording directly over my shoulder. "Hey, watch it!" I barked.

He stumbled back, trying to get out of the way. "M-my apologies!"

"Is he going to be okay?" asked a familiar voice from

behind. I turned to see Abigail standing in the archway, watching us.

I paused, surprised to see her. Had she followed us here? Was her guilt still so strong that she needed reassurance?

Athena chimed in with an answer before I could. "He will recover soon. His injury was moderately life-threatening."

"See?" I said, looking at Abigail. "Only moderately. The kid will be fine."

Octavia looked at me and Abigail, then wheeled herself away from the pod. "If the Constable is all set, I'd like to see to something. Hitchens, Bolin, if the two of you don't mind."

"Oh?" asked Hitchens.

Octavia motioned at the back of her chair.

"Ah, yes, of course," said the good doctor. He grabbed the handles and began to wheel her away.

Bolin followed with them, and I watched the three head into the corridor, toward the elevator.

Abigail approached, giving me a nod, then leaned close enough to see inside the pod, staring at the boy inside. She touched the glass, and I could see in her eyes how real the fear had been.

Maybe she didn't even know it herself, but there it was, behind those beautiful green eyes. A dreadful sort of fear that wasn't expected, the kind you didn't see coming. It was a surprise when you felt it, and the shock stayed with you until it was done, and you wondered why you never saw it before. You wondered how you could let it get this far.

Abigail had treated this kid like garbage ever since she first met him. It was hate that did it to her. Hate for the Union, for the people who did those awful things to Lex, back in that lab.

I knew what it was like to have hate like that…to want a person dead because of what they represented. I knew it better than most, I wagered, and maybe that was why I could so easily see the remorse that followed.

Because I knew what it meant to be afraid of myself…

Afraid of what so much hate might do to me.

12

Alphonse cracked his eyes open and blinked several times, trying to focus. He licked his lips, swallowing hard.

"Welcome back," I said, standing beside his pod. I was alone in the med bay, except for the Constable himself. Abigail had left only a few minutes ago but would be back soon.

"Where...?" muttered Alphonse, clearly confused about what was going on.

"You took a bad hit in the chest. The bullet was lodged near an artery, but we got it out," I explained. "Congrats. You get to live."

"That's a relief," he said, trying to smile.

"Are you in a lot of pain?" I asked.

He pushed himself up, trying to straighten his back. "It's manageable. Thank you, Captain."

"Don't thank me," I said, fanning a hand at him. "I didn't do anything."

He tried to laugh at my humility, only to cough instead.

"You're an idiot for doing what you did," I said after a short moment of silence. "You almost died because of it."

"I couldn't let that woman die," he said, giving me that same innocent expression I had grown accustomed to by now. Alphonse had never struck me as a Constable, not in the way I imagined them to be. He knew how to fight, sure, but he always looked so innocent, like he was just a kid, confused about what he was doing here. Being next to him had felt familiar, like talking with an old friend. At first, I'd thought it was a tactic to gain my trust, but now I was beginning to believe otherwise. Maybe this was just his personality. Maybe he really was just a kind person.

"You risked your life to save Abigail," I said, resting my hand on the side of the pod. "She treated you like crap."

"She had a good reason," he said. "She was trying to protect a child."

The way he said it felt genuine, like he really believed it.

"I must admit, I was concerned the bullet might have set off the bomb you gave me," he continued, chuckling a little.

"There never was a bomb, Al. Didn't you figure that out already?" I asked.

It was true. As much as I wasn't sure about Alphonse at the time, putting a bomb inside his gut had simply been a bluff. Athena had explained that such a surgery would be too difficult, especially given how little power *Titan* had at the time. I figured bluffing would be enough to keep him in line, and besides, I was a quick shot...and he didn't have a gun.

"I was pretty certain you were lying," he answered. "Although one never knows about these things."

I nodded. "You're welcome."

"For what?" he asked.

"Not blowing you up," I said.

He smiled. "You're always joking."

"What's your deal, Al? What do you have to gain from helping any of us? Tell me the truth now, would you? I know there's more going on inside that stupid head of yours than you've let on."

He managed a laugh this time, but only a small one. "You have to understand, Captain. While I might have wanted to assist you, I am still a Constable. I couldn't be certain you were in the right, not until I had enough data." He cleared his throat. "I read about Lex when I was working in the Red Tower. It's where the Constables keep all classified records. I'd heard about the experiments from a fellow of mine, someone you might call an associate, but not a friend. She had mentioned some interesting work being done in the Third Laboratory."

"The Third Laboratory?" I asked. "Is that the name of the place Lex was being held?"

He nodded. "The very same. I located the files, which are on a closed system, meaning you can't access them outside of the facility. I began to read about the work being done, and as I am prone to do, I became obsessed. I wanted to know everything there was to know about the children."

"Children?" I asked. "How many were there? Did they all have tattoos like Lex?"

"No, not quite, although it wasn't for lack of trying," he said. "Upon their discovery of the child, they began working on a means of replicating the markings. Several children were used as test subjects, each for different reasons. Thousands of tests were attempted, all of which resulted in utter failure, as you may have already guessed."

"Failure? Does that mean the other kids…?"

"I'm afraid so, Captain," said Alphonse. "I can't begin to imagine how many were lost. Even after the girl was taken, the Union continued their attempts at replicating her abilities, none of which has been successful, last I checked."

"How many?" I asked in a low growl.

He paused. "Hundreds. Maybe more."

I stared at him in disbelief, trying to imagine so many kids, all of them gone. I couldn't wrap my head around it. The thought was unimaginable.

"To tell you the truth, Captain, I wasn't certain whether or not you were any better," Alphonse added. "Not until I was able to observe you for myself."

"Observe?" I asked, coming out of my thoughts. "The way I remember it, we took you prisoner and stuck you in a cell. Are you telling me that was all part of the plan?"

"It went a bit messier than I expected, because of

Docker, as you'll recall. I only wanted to see whether you could be trusted with the girl."

"And if I couldn't?" I asked, raising my eye. "I seem to recall shoving a pistol in your face...more than once."

"I knew you wouldn't shoot me. You aren't the type to shoot an unarmed man," he said.

"You make a lot of assumptions," I told him.

"No," he said. "I research. You'd be surprised what you can find in the Tower's database. They have profiles on all of you."

"Is that so?" I asked with a smirk.

"You're an honorable man, Captain Hughes, whether you want to admit it or not," said the Constable.

I scoffed. "Shove it up your ass, Al."

I WALKED out of the lift, on my way back from the med bay, when I saw Octavia. She was alone, wheeling herself along. I gave her a nod and asked, "Where's the professor?"

"Helping Bolin clear out one of the rooms so that Camilla can have her own space," she said.

Camilla and her father had been sharing a room since we arrived. We'd all been restricted to using the main deck, but now with power being restored, several rooms seemed to have opened up. "Are you going to check on Alphonse?" I asked.

"Hardly," she said. "Athena says she can unlock that medical supply closet. I thought I'd have a look."

"Supply closet? Wouldn't all that stuff be expired by now?" I asked.

"Not everything," she said. "This ship was meant to travel for generations. They went through the trouble of securing quite a bit of their medicine in stasis."

"If the power was out on that floor, how could it maintain the supplies?" I asked.

"Power reserves," Athena chimed in. Her disembodied voice made both of us flinch. "Pardon the interruption, Captain, but to answer your question, there are several emergency systems tied directly to the backup power supply. There is a priority tree in place to ensure the essentials remain online at all times."

"Well, there you go," said Octavia, wheeling herself past me. "I'll do an inventory and let you know what we have. Hopefully, there's something worthwhile."

She boarded the elevator and I watched as the doors closed.

"Captain," said Athena. "If I might have a word."

"What is it?" I asked.

"I believe we have a situation that requires your immediate attention." She blipped into existence, manifesting beside me in her physical form.

My hand went straight to my pistol, quickly relaxing. "Godsdammit."

"I'm detecting movement headed towards our current

coordinates. I believe it is a Union ship, quite large, along with multiple other vessels."

"A large ship?" I asked. My mind went to the worst possible scenario.

She nodded. "We've seen it before. The *Galactic Dawn*."

My eyes widened at the sound of the name. "The *Dawn*? Are you sure?"

"I can't confirm it precisely, but given its size and shape, it is extremely likely," she said.

"Looks like we're still not free of this mess," I said. "Do we have enough time to run?"

"They'll arrive within a few minutes. I apologize for not informing you sooner, but my long-range sensors could not detect them until power was restored."

I felt heat in my cheeks, a rising tension in my throat. "Tell the others to meet me in the landing bay," I said. "Prime whatever weapons you've got and get ready to make the jump to slipspace."

"Understood, Captain," said the Cognitive.

She suddenly vanished, leaving me alone in the hall. I began running, faster and faster, headed to my ship, hoping I still had enough time.

13

EVERYONE ARRIVED IN THE HANGAR, including the kids. I was already in the *Star*, prepping the ship to launch if it needed to.

I tapped my ear. "Siggy, patch me through to the others outside."

"Of course, sir," said the A.I. "Please speak when ready."

I cleared my throat. "In case Athena forgot to tell you folks, Brigham is on his way. He'll be here any minute," I explained.

"On his way?" asked Abigail, who was standing beside Freddie and Hitchens.

Bolin tilted his head. "Is this the man who's been chasing you? The general?"

"That's the guy," I said. "He's coming to get us, along

with multiple other ships. Athena's prepping the slip engine, but she needs a bit of time. The new core hasn't fully integrated yet."

"What does that mean for the rest of us?" asked Octavia.

"It means we have to stall," I said. "Athena, can you hear me?"

"Yes, Captain," said the Cognitive.

"I'm taking the *Star* out to drop a few dozen mines right in front of us. We'll create a tunnel and they'll have no choice but to go through the bombs," I explained.

"What can we do to help?" asked Abigail.

"This is a one-man job. The rest of you stay here while Siggy and I handle things on the outside." I strapped myself into my chair and began the engine prep.

"You can't just expect the rest of us to wait here while you run off alone," said Abigail.

"Why not? It's not like I need you to help me drop a couple of bombs," I said.

"Someone needs to handle the guns while you're dropping bombs," she said.

"I can handle both. I've done it before."

She stormed up to the ship. "Sigmond, open the godsdamn door!"

"Acknowledged," said Sigmond.

The lift door dropped slowly to the floor. "Godsdammit, Siggy!" I barked. "You aren't supposed to take orders from anyone but me!"

"Apologies, sir, but Ms. Pryar was rather insistent," he said.

Abigail climbed inside and began jogging to the cockpit. I closed the lift and primed my engines. "Everyone else, get inside and wait for us to get back!"

"See you in a bit," said Bolin.

"Try not to die," said Octavia.

Abigail banged on my door and I opened it. She shuffled inside and took the seat next to me, strapping herself in. "I can't believe you almost left me here, Jace."

"I didn't want you to take the risk," I said.

She snapped her eyes at me, scowling. "It doesn't matter what you want. All that matters is what's best for the team! You running off on your own isn't *that*. It's the opposite. What happens if you get yourself killed?"

I sighed. "I can't win for trying."

"And you never will as long as I'm here," she said.

The *Renegade Star* lifted off *Titan*'s deck and made its way into clear space, leaving the others behind. They'd be safe for now, so long as we could plant the bombs and stall.

Long enough so *Titan* could open that tunnel and get the hell out of here.

THE SLIP TUNNEL opened while we were still deploying the bombs, and the first of several ships entered the system. It wasn't the *Galactic Dawn*, though, but another Union military ship with credentials I didn't recognize. "Captain Jace Hughes of the *Renegade Star*, you are under arrest for the abduction of—"

I cut the transmission off. "Shut the hell up," I said, knowing they couldn't hear me. I dropped the last of the mines in place. The little black bomb slid out of my ship and into open space, bringing itself to a motionless standstill.

"Do you really think this will be enough to slow down those ships?" asked Abigail.

"Without a doubt," I said, pulling us back from the line of explosives that currently surrounded *Titan*.

"Sir," interjected Sigmond. "Please be advised. The incoming vessel is charging weapons."

"Raise shields!" I snapped.

A blast struck our side, but the shields took most of the damage.

"Idiots," I muttered. "They'll hit these mines if they aren't careful."

I brought us around, turning my targeting sights on the enemy spacecraft. Abigail grabbed the controls and locked on, firing a spread the moment she had the chance.

The enemy ship came flying in our direction, right as several others began to emerge from the tunnel. Before I could say anything else, another rift formed in the nearby space. It was a separate tunnel from the last, which meant even more reinforcements. "Sensors detect a Sarkonian vessel incoming," informed Siggy.

I wanted to curse. I hadn't expected so many of them this soon. "Start firing!" I barked at Abigail, flying us in a 90-degree angle, away from the mines and the oncoming ship.

We dove, avoiding the shots. The other ship followed, and for a brief moment, I considered trying to lure them closer to the mine field but stopped myself. It wouldn't do any good to waste the bombs on a ship that small. We needed those for the big gun, the *Galactic Dawn* itself, which still hadn't arrived.

Athena's voice came in over the com. "Captain, engines are online. I'm forming the slip tunnel now. Please return to *Titan* immediately."

"Give me just a godsdamn second!" I yelled, pulling on the control stick.

We moved around the other fighter and Abigail kept suppressing fire on it, hitting its shields repeatedly.

"Siggy, what's the status of that ship?" I asked.

"Analyzing. The vessel is using a standard mid-tier shield. Two direct hits with a quad cannon should disable it."

"Hear that?" I asked, glancing at Abby. "Make it count!"

She nodded, then turned back and took aim, sweeping her hand over the targeting holo on the dash. She fired the first quad cannon, missing the enemy vessel.

Abby cursed, narrowing her eyes, and tried again. This time, the torpedo struck the ship, and I heard her breathe a sigh of relief. She quickly followed it up with another. The combined strength of the two blasts was enough to crack the shield.

I took us in closer. "Again!" I shouted.

She leaned forward, clutching the stick, and lit up the godsdamn ship with a spray of shots. Multiple rounds penetrated the hull, ripping it nearly in half and igniting the engines. The ship exploded in a wicked blast just as we turned back towards the mines.

Without missing a beat, the other ships began to move towards the field, each one activating shields and weapons. They weren't about to let *Titan* leave, not without doing everything they could to stop it.

The lead ship in the fleet—a small Union vessel similar to the one where we'd originally found Alphonse—snagged a mine as soon as it entered the area. The explosion obliterated the small craft, splitting it into hundreds, if not thousands, of pieces. The rest of the fleet stayed back, finally realizing that there were bombs waiting for them.

In seconds, they began firing missiles into the mine field, trying to clear a path. It seemed to work, albeit slowly, as the torpedoes began colliding with the mines, one at a time.

We had created three hexagon layers of mines between the fleet and *Titan*, which was the most effective area of coverage we could establish in such a short amount of time. It wouldn't take the fleet very long to break through, but Athena only needed a few moments.

Titan's beams formed at its center, ripping a tear in space, creating a new tunnel. The process was fast and, within seconds, the opening had been formed.

"That's our cue," I said. "Siggy, move us—"

Before I could finish, I felt the entire ship toss sideways, like we'd been hit.

"What was that?!" I asked.

"Our shields are taking heavy fire, sir," informed Sigmond. "We can't sustain this for long."

"Who the hell is it now?" I asked. The holo switched to show me a Sarkonian ship in pursuit, firing rapidly at us. It was way too close for comfort.

Abigail swiveled in her seat. "Should we run?"

"Not until we take it down!" I barked.

"If we're not careful, we'll be stuck without a shield!" she returned.

"We can't let them follow us back to *Titan*," I said.

I brought the ship around and targeted the Sarkonian vessel. Abigail hit the ship with a spread, but it didn't seem to slow it down. "Sir, I am detecting movement on the surface of the enemy vessel," said Sigmond.

"What kind of movement?" I asked.

"I believe they are deploying a weapon," he said.

The holo showed part of the Sarkonian ship sliding back into the hull, revealing some kind of cannon. "What the hell is that?" I asked.

"Firing torpedoes!" snapped Abigail.

The quad cannons landed a direct hit on the other ship,

but before we could congratulate ourselves, something struck the side of our hull.

The *Renegade Star* shook, forcing me into my harness. "What was that?"

"Enemy ship has been immobilized," said Sigmond.

"That's not what I asked, godsdammit!" I said.

Abby touched the dash and pulled up a sensor analysis of the hull. "It looks like there's something on the side of the ship," she said.

I zoomed in on the object, which was glowing red against the blue outline of our hull. "Siggy, run a scan on that thing. See what it is."

"Analyzing..." said the A.I. "Object appears to be a neutron bomb, primed for remote detonation."

"Did he just say a bomb?" asked Abigail.

"He did," I said, pulling the control sticks back and setting us in the opposite direction. "We need to get away from the other ships here, before one of them shoots at us and sets that thing off."

"Should we dock inside *Titan*?" she asked.

I shook my head. "We can't take it inside the ship, not until we get it removed." I tabbed the control, activating the com. "Athena, you picking this up?"

"Affirmative," she said.

"Take the tunnel. We'll be right behind you. Got a little business to take care of."

"Are you certain?" asked Athena. "What's delaying your arrival? Do you need assistance?"

"We're packing a bomb on our back. I can't risk this thing getting back to you."

"Captain, I must insist that you not—"

"Just do as I say and go!"

"As you wish," said Athena. "I shall send our next destination to Sigmond. Please accept."

"Coordinates received," said Sigmond.

"Hear that?" I asked. "We got them. Now get out of here! We'll meet you there!"

"Acknowledged, Captain. Good luck," said Athena.

Several of the enemy ships began to move toward *Titan*. The moon-sized vessel eased its way into the newly created slip tunnel, gradually disappearing inside, until it was fully immersed. The other ships entered the minefield, determined not to let *Titan* escape.

While the fleet was distracted with their suicidal mission to reclaim Lex, I set our coordinates on another tunnel, near the end of the system.

The *Renegade Star* took off away from the fleet, putting as much space between us and them as possible. My ship wasn't the fastest in the galaxy, but with all of them so distracted, we might actually stand a chance at getting out of here.

I unhooked my harness. "Stay here and keep us on target," I said, getting to my feet. I hit the switch to open the door and started to leave.

"Where do you think you're going?" asked Abigail.

"In case you already forgot, we've got a bomb on our ass. Somebody has to take care of it."

"By yourself?" she asked. "How are you going to——"

I took off running down the corridor. "I'll call you on the com when I'm outside!" I yelled over my shoulder.

I took the turn in the hall and went straight into the cargo bay. The lockers were already open, so I snagged one of the suits and began getting dressed.

"Siggy, how long before our shields are reactivated?" I asked, sliding my arms through the sleeves.

"The Sarkonian ship used an electromagnetic charge to disrupt the polarity of our shield. The effects are temporary. Partial power will be restored within thirty seconds," answered the A.I.

"Perfect," I said, securing my waist. "Establish shields as soon as possible then drop them on my mark."

"As you wish, sir."

I locked my helmet into place, then activated my oxygen tank. The cool taste of air entered my helmet, and I heard the echo of my own breathing. I was suddenly much more aware of how fast my heart was pounding. "Godsdammit," I muttered. "The trouble I find."

ONCE THE SHIELD WAS ESTABLISHED, I was out the lift, using my boots to magnetically grip the hull as I moved, one slow step at a time, toward the bomb.

The bomb, which, as it happened, was snug and secure inside the section just above my bedroom. If this thing ended up damaging my quarters, I was going to be royally pissed.

"Abigail, do you hear me?" I asked, activating my com.

"I do!" she responded with hardly any static overlaying her voice.

I took another step, letting the magnet in my boot fully grab the hull before moving again. "I'm almost at the bomb. Stay focused on getting us to the tunnel."

"We'll be there in…six minutes," she said.

"We might have to sit there for a few while I get this detached, but we'll make it," I said, taking another step.

I could already see the lump in my hull, resting several meters near the center of the *Renegade Star*. It looked like a piece of cancer, a foreign hunk of poison that didn't belong.

I edged my way forward, increasingly more aware of the danger I was putting myself in. Every step brought me closer to a godsdamn bomb.

I stepped across the airlock, careful not to touch the glass window, since it wasn't metal and the last thing I needed was to lose my footing.

"Sir, a more thorough examination of the device has revealed a small problem," said Sigmond.

"What is it now?" I asked. The bomb was only two meters away. I was nearly there.

"The casing itself is standard Sarkonian polymetal,

while the locking mechanism and panel is Neutronium-plated, making it difficult to open. It may be best to dislodge the device manually, rather than disarm it."

"You're saying I can't open it?" I asked.

"That is correct."

I made an audible growl. "You're killing me, Siggy."

"Apologies, sir. That is the opposite of my intention."

I sighed, taking the last step, then bent down so I was half-a-meter beside the bomb. I retrieved a small pack that I'd attached to my side, removing the thermal saw from inside. "Time for some last-minute surgery."

THREE MINUTES into this and I was already pretty sure I was going to accidentally blow up my ship.

I used the thermal saw to heat the hull and slowly soften the areas around the bomb.

Sweat dripped down off my forehead, landing inside my suit. It was like a sauna all of a sudden. Was I seriously this nervous?

My hands kept shaking, so I figured I must be. Still, I didn't let it stop me from doing the job. It's not like anyone else was going to come along and save us. It was up to me.

I smirked at the thought. I'd told Camilla the same thing not that long ago. The universe was a shitstorm, and the only person you can rely on is yourself. Maybe that was true, but Abigail was inside at this very minute, handling the controls. She didn't have to be here with me on this idiotic mission. She'd chosen to come along with me...to put herself out on the front line.

I rolled my eyes. *All that means is that we're both idiots,* I thought, a slight grin on my face. *But still, better to be fools together than dead and alone.*

I continued to melt the metal around the bottom of the bomb, edging it away from the hull, one centimeter at a time.

"Jace, we're almost at the tunnel," said Abigail over the com. "How long before you're back inside?"

"I'm still dealing with it. Hold on," I said.

"Understood," she answered.

I grabbed the side of the bomb and pulled it, trying to yank the back of it free of the ship. One of the blinking lights changed from green to orange, a first since I'd come up here. "What the—"

"The bomb is charging, sir," said Sigmond. "Please, be advised. The bomb is—"

"Fuck!" I snapped, pulling it off the last of the melted hull. "Siggy, get ready to drop the shield as soon as I tell you!"

"Yes, sir," he answered.

I gripped the explosive with both hands, pulling it off the hull. It refused to come up all the way, since it was still attached by a thin piece of soft metal. I squatted, pushing against the ship, and pulled the device with every ounce of strength I could muster. The resistance I felt suddenly ended, and I nearly fell backwards.

I twisted where I stood, lifting the bomb to my chest and aiming it toward the rear of the *Renegade Star*. "Now, Siggy! Drop the shields!"

The area around the ship flickered. "Shields are down, sir," said Sigmond.

"Here we go!" I shouted, throwing the megaton bomb away from me. It floated away, still headed in the same direction we were currently flying, but slightly off course, thanks to my push.

"Excellent work, sir," said Sigmond.

"Thanks, Siggy," I said, letting myself breathe. "Raise the shields as soon as that thing is out of our—"

The bomb exploded before I could finish. The ship tossed instantly, and I felt the force of the blast as it knocked me free of the hull. I went spiraling into the void, away from the *Star*, unable to right my angle.

I tried to say something…to call Abby and ask if she was okay…to ask Siggy if the ship was still intact.

Most of all, I just tried to keep my eyes open.

14

I FELT a hand around my wrist, pulling me from the bed. I wasn't surprised, because I could hear my father coming, stomping on the old wood floors as he marched to get me. Even before he was there, I could already smell the liquor.

"Up and at 'em, Jacey," said the old man. "I got somethin' I wanna show ya."

I hopped on one foot as he dragged me through my bedroom, towards the door, and into the main sitting room.

I already knew what this was about. I'd heard him yelling at my mom a few hours ago before he went to the bar. He wanted to leave and head out to join Uncle Teddy, up on Talos, the nearest colony to Epsy. There were prospects, he had told her. My dad was always talking about prospects.

He stumbled before we reached the couch, his foot

catching on the dislodged plank in the floor. "Gods-dammit!" he shouted. "I forgot to fix that. Why didn't you remind me about the damn plank?"

He'd been meaning to fix that for three months now but still hadn't found the time.

I sat down on the couch, while my dad slammed his big ass down on the stool in front of me. I could see his pistol on his hip, the same one he'd carried at his side since he was sixteen. The same one that, as he'd told me, killed over forty men. "Your momma says I ain't got what it takes, Jacey," said the overweight dust miner. "She says there ain't no more upward momentum for folks like us. Wattayou think about that?"

"Why would Momma say that?" I asked, believing him instantly.

"She don't know nuthin' about nuthin', Jacey. That woman is small-time." He coughed into his fist, gray spit hitting his fingers. "You and me, we got better stuff in us, don't we? We're gonna be Renegades and get ourselves a hot life!"

"Yeah!" I exclaimed, excited at the sound of the word. My father had recently started telling me about Renegades and how wonderful their lives were. He said they all had ships and traveled all over the galaxy, doing whatever they wanted. If you were a Renegade, my father would always say, you can have it all.

"Damn planet's going to hell and I'm smart enough to

see which way the wind is headed. You know what I'm saying, Jacey?" he asked.

I nodded. "It stinks!"

He laughed. "Your momma, she's a simple one. She don't see it. You do, though, don't you, Jacey?"

I nodded again. "Yeah, Pop! It stinks bad!" I plugged my nose, trying to demonstrate.

He stared at me, a stupid expression on his face, like he was lost for a moment, but then he smirked. "That's right. You get it. Of course my kid gets it." He smacked my knee with his burly hand. My father gave me a grin, his lips crooked and red. "Guess what I got in my pocket, Jacey," he said, reaching to show me before I could even give him an answer. I heard a rustle of something, then he pulled out a small piece of paper, dangling it in my face. "You know what this is?" he asked. "It's a ticket. A special ticket, like the kind we always talked about."

My eyes widened. "You got a ticket to space?" I asked, dropping my jaw. "No way!"

He shoved it in my face, clumsily hitting me in the fore-head, although I didn't care. I was too busy trying to see what the ticket said on it.

CLASS – STD
TICKET TIME – 3PM DAY
ADULT – ONE
FROM – VERNIN, EPSY
TO – ARENSDALE, TALOS

"See it?" he asked, trying to hold it steady. "Now we can do what we always wanted, Jacey."

"Whoa!" I exclaimed.

He smiled. "Our times in this shithole are over. Won't be long before everyone from the Union to Sarkonia is talkin' 'bout the Hughes boys. Ain't that right?"

"Ain't no one better than a Hughes!" I shouted, reciting the phrase my father would often say when comparing our family.

He began to laugh but coughed instead. "You're funny," he said, clearing his throat and wheezing. All those years in the mines had done my father no favors.

"When can we go?" I asked, smiling. "How long before we get to be Renegades?"

He snickered. "You're funny, Jacey. I can't take no kid with me to Talos. I need to get up there on my own so I can get a good job."

I frowned but knew I shouldn't. My father would never leave me behind if he didn't have to. I knew that.

"Don't worry, Jacey. You'll just wait around here for a while. I gotta get a good job first, but then it won't take me long to get you a ticket too." He paused for a second. "And your momma. She don't get our dream now, but she will. Just you wait."

"Okay, Pop. I'll wait here and be good," I said, trying to act tough.

He grinned. "Won't take me more than a month, I bet! Maybe less if I can work those bigwigs on the shuttle." He tried to wink at me but blinked both eyes instead. "Gonna be tough, but just you wait, Jacey. I'm gonna make it big out there!"

I heard a knock at the front door, and my father flinched, startled by the sound. "That must be…" He looked at me. "Uh…sorry, kid, but I gotta get going now if I'm gonna make the flight tomorrow. Gotta travel all the way to Vernin City. Remember when we went there a few years ago?"

Another bang on the door. "Hello?" called a man. "Someone call about a ride?"

My father got to his feet. "Be right there!" he barked, and in a softer voice, he said, "Sorry to go like this, Jacey, but I'll see you real soon, got it?"

"Got it," I echoed, trying to keep my smile.

I watched him head to the door then pause to look at me. His eyes lingered on me for a moment, a distant expression on his face—one I didn't recognize. Then he smiled at me with the same charming grin he always had. "Someday, you're gonna learn, Jacey…what it means to be a man. Someday, you're gonna know what it feels like to be me."

He smacked his chest and closed the door.

Off to better prospects.

"Jace," a faint voice called.

I stirred in my suit.

"Jace!"

My eyes broke open, and I was suddenly gasping. "Gods!" I snapped, instantly confused about where I was and how I'd gotten there. "Holy godsdamn hell!"

"Jace, are you okay?!" shouted a woman in my ear.

It took me a second to realize who the hell this person was. "Abby?" I said, trying to get my bearings. I turned my head as much as I could, only to realize that I was trapped inside a godsdamn spacesuit. *Oh, right,* I thought, remembering the thing about the bomb.

"Don't worry, I'll bring the ship back around to you," said Abby.

"I'm afraid that may prove difficult," interjected Sigmond.

"What do you mean?" I asked.

"Our thrusters were damaged in the blast," he explained. "We are only operating at 30 percent. It will take several minutes to retrieve you. I do apologize, sir."

"I'm not going anywhere, but you'd better move your asses," I said.

I was still spinning from the blast, so I reached for my arm control panel and activated my suit's stabilizers, attached on the left and right shoulders. Each compartment only contained a small amount of compressed nitrogen to correct my velocity, which meant it was only for emergencies. I supposed this counted, then tapped the command to activate the unit.

The gas released in spurts, a little at a time, gradually

killing my momentum until I was mostly immobilized. No more spinning, no more spiraling in a random direction. I still had enough gas to help me turn around or send me flying in another direction, should I need it.

I couldn't see the *Renegade Star* yet, but I didn't expect to in so much darkness. Space was vast and empty, with only stars to guide your path. I wouldn't be able to spot my own ship until it was right up on me. *Titan* might have been a different story, but that ship was long gone now, completely out of reach.

"Sir, I am detecting multiple incoming vessels, breaking off from the fleet," said Sigmond.

"Strike ships? How many?" I asked, staring in the direction of the fleet. I couldn't see anything, not even the bigger ships, but that didn't keep me from trying.

"Eight, sir," he responded.

The *Renegade Star* could handle two, maybe three strike ships, but eight? Not a godsdamn chance. "How long until they get here?"

"Two minutes," said the A.I.

"And how long before you pick me up?" I asked.

"Three minutes," he answered.

I bit the inside of my mouth, twisting my lip as I continued to watch the void in front of me, towards the system's sun, which shone with an intensity I was only just noticing. A white glow, much like one on Epsy. "Siggy," I said, after a moment. "Open a tunnel. I want you to take Abigail to the coordinates Athena gave you."

Abigail answered before the A.I. could respond. "Jace, what are you talking about? We're not leaving you behind. Don't be an idiot!"

I ignored her. "Siggy, you do as I say. Understand? Captain's orders. Don't make me use the godsdamn command password on you."

"Siggy, don't listen to that fool! We're not leaving him here," insisted Abigail.

"Sir, are you certain?" asked Sigmond. "A quick analysis concludes that there is still an 8 percent chance of success, should we continue on our present course to procure you."

I smirked. "I appreciate the optimism, Siggy, but get that fat ass of yours in gear and go. Your priority now is to protect the nun. You got it?"

"Jace!" shouted Abigail. "You can't just order me to leave you behind! Don't be such a—"

I cut the com off. She was probably screaming at the console right now, but oh well. It was for her own good.

THE UNION SQUADRON of strike ships arrived shortly after I gave the order to leave. They came to a quick halt right in front of me, so close I could see them and they could see me.

I knew they wouldn't shoot me, not without first dragging me into a prison cell and interrogating me for information. I wasn't stupid enough to think otherwise.

That didn't mean I wouldn't kill as many of these fools as possible in the process, though. If they wanted to take me in alive, it was going to cost them. That was for damn sure.

The nearest strike ship moved in, closing the gap between us, until it was hovering a hundred yards away. It could have been less or more. Hard to tell in space.

The side hatch of the ship opened, its door sliding up to reveal two men, each wearing a spacesuit. One of them pointed toward me then pointed at the ship. I guessed he was trying to tell me to come inside, but I wasn't about to make this easy for them. That asshole would have to come and get me first.

After a few fruitless attempts to communicate, he seemed to say something to the person beside him, and the two leapt free of the ship and headed in my direction.

When they were about halfway to me, I reached for my wrist and tabbed the thruster controls, turning myself around. With my back at them, I burst forward, floating away. With my momentum set, I used the last of my nitrogen to twist myself around so I could see them and then waved.

The two men stopped where they were, doubling back to their ship. "That's right, you little fuck nuggets," I muttered. "You want me, you're gonna have to work for it."

Three of the ships came closer, gaining quickly on me. Each of their doors opened this time, rather than just one, and I saw several suited individuals emerge, each ready to take me in.

That was more like it.

I continued floating away from them, toward the empty void at my back. It was satisfying, watching them squirm. I expected I'd get the beating of my life in a few minutes, once they had me inside one of their ships...but damn if it wasn't worth it.

Right as three of the soldiers were getting close to me, with one angry-looking asshole at the forefront, something happened.

A green glow came over us, which I could see reflecting off their helmets and suits, coming from behind me.

The soldiers stopped where they were, motioning to each other to return to their ships. They scurried like crabs on a beach, a mad panic in them.

To make matters worse, the glow had grown stronger and brighter. It was beginning to encapsulate my own suit. I raised my arm, trying to look at the reflection of the tiny dash on my wrist.

A split in space had formed, creating an opening to slip-space. The swirling emerald shined brightly against my plating.

That was when the ship emerged, its massive circular hull squeezing through the lightning walls. At first, I didn't recognize it. The panel on my wrist was lousy for viewing, with its dents and smudged surface, but after a moment, I began to piece together what I was seeing.

It was *Titan*, coming back to the fight.

One of the strike ships burst forward, towards me, probably in a last-ditch effort to pick me up, but before it could get too close, a ray of blue light overtook us.

Nearly all of the strike ships were caught inside of it, along with me. I began to drift upwards, away from the enemy ships, which seemed to be totally motionless. The ship that had been on its way to me was frozen in place, immobilized and unable to either attack or flee.

Meanwhile, I continued to move at a 45-degree angle, the blue light encapsulating me as it brought me closer to the source.

Closer to *Titan*.

Realizing my com was still turned off, I switched it back on. "Hello? Anyone reading me?" I asked.

"Welcome, Captain Hughes," answered Athena. "I apologize for the delay."

"What are you doing here?" I asked. "I thought I told you to run."

"I did as you asked but changed the plan mid-flight. I shifted the tunnel to curve back to the edge of the system, hoping to assist the *Renegade Star*."

"Where's Abigail? Did she get away?" I asked.

"I sent a command to Sigmond the moment we arrived. He was in the process of opening a tunnel not far from our present location," she explained. "Ms. Pryar should return momentarily."

I let the beam carry me deeper into the megastructure.

It only took a minute or so before I was brought inside one of the docking bays—different from the one the *Star* typically parked in. I floated over the floor, the blue light surrounding me, and gently came to a rest, right on my ass.

I got to my feet and, before I could say anything, a display appeared on the nearby wall, showing the ships outside, still trapped in the beam. "Captain," said Athena, appearing in the corner of the screen. "What would you prefer I do with these vessels?"

I briefly considered telling her to slam them together until each of the strike ships was nothing but a piece of metal with flattened Union soldiers between them, but then decided against it.

Not because I didn't want to. I would've loved to watch those assholes get what they deserved. It was just that we had to get our asses out of here before the rest of that fleet caught up with us. They must have certainly noticed *Titan* by now, so it wouldn't be long before they were all over us. "Let's head out. Open a new tunnel, and as soon as the *Star* is here, set a course and get us out of this godsforsaken system." I twisted my helmet, snapping it off. "And, Athena, one last thing."

"Yes, Captain?" she asked.

"If any of those strike ships tries anything, use one of those heavy cannons of yours and blow them straight to hell. Don't leave a scrap of metal behind."

15

THE *RENEGADE STAR* docked a few minutes after I was back on *Titan*. The second it landed, we were already pushing into a new tunnel, well on our way to anywhere-but-here.

Abigail found me a few minutes later. I could see she was steaming before she even got to me. "Jace Hughes! How *dare* you force me to leave you behind! Do you have some sort of death wish?!" She marched straight up to me, sticking her finger in my face. "You can't just throw your life away and expect the rest of us to let you do it! What sort of idiot are you? Answer me, godsdammit!"

I stared at her as she glared up at me. "You sure let yourself get worked up, don't you?" I asked.

"Don't try to change the subject! I could have handled those ships! You can't just make all the decisions, Jace! So what if I'm in danger? You don't give yourself up to save me!"

I started to walk past her, towards the *Star*. "Who said I was saving you?" I asked. "Do you have any idea how long it took me to save up the cash to buy this ship? It'd take ages to get a new one."

She let out an angry snarl, which made me chuckle. "You're hopeless!"

I climbed aboard my ship and sealed the lift so I wouldn't be disturbed.

"Welcome back, sir," said Sigmond. "I'm relieved to see you're still alive."

"Thanks, Siggy," I said, taking a sip of my drink. It burned the part of my lip that I'd chewed, but I didn't care. "Athena, you hearing me?"

"Yes, Captain," she answered.

"I want to be alone for a few hours. Don't bother me unless you have to." I paused. "Don't bother me at all. Bother Freddie or something."

"If you wish," she answered.

I grabbed a bottle of whiskey and collapsed in my sofa, pouring myself a drink and putting my feet up.

I raised my cup. "Here's to nearly getting caught and killed, Siggy."

"Here, here," said Sigmond.

I lowered the cup, staring down at the swirling liquid. "Here, here," I muttered, but didn't take another drink. Instead, I sat it on the table in front of me and watched it. I stared into it, although I couldn't say why. I started to reach for it, but dropped my hand to my side instead. For some reason, I just didn't want it anymore.

I MANAGED to fall asleep pretty quickly, all the energy drained from me. When I finally awoke, it was the early morning, which meant I'd slept for nearly ten hours.

I showered and pissed, then tossed my jacket on and holstered my gun on my hip.

No doubt, everyone was probably still asleep. It would be the perfect time to take a walk and stretch my legs.

"Enjoy your stroll, sir," said Sigmond.

I shot him a rude gesture as I exited the ship then made my way into the nearby corridor.

The sleeping quarters for the rest of the crew were along this hallway and one other, which allowed each of them to stay in close proximity should anything need their collective attention. The only exceptions were me and Dressler, who was still on my ship in Abigail's old room.

It had been my idea originally to have everyone's quarters nearby. We'd encountered an alarming number of emergency situations before now, so we'd be stupid not to expect more of them, as today had proven. The closer their rooms, the faster they'd be able to mobilize, or so the hope had been. You can never predict how anyone will react in an emergency—not until it actually happens.

Titan had a cafeteria, which used long-term stasis pods to keep various amenities intact, including meals and drinks. There were far less now than when *Titan* had first switched to emergency power, two thousand years ago, and many of the pods had stopped working by this point. Still, we had enough food and water to keep us going for the next three centuries. There were only eight of us, after all.

I entered the cafeteria and walked up to the dispenser, pressing the button I knew produced a hot plate of eggs and bacon. It arrived in less than a minute, steaming and smelling like the real thing, although I knew it was simply reprocessed organic matter, adapted to fit a certain kind of taste and texture.

I took my seat in one of the ten, thirty-seat benches, and had a bite. *Not bad for a two-thousand-year-old omelet,* I thought.

It sort of reminded me of the food in juvie, back on Epsy. They used to feed the kids there the same meals every week, most of which was disgusting variations of the same soy compilation. Breakfast was different, though, because it was hard to mess up eggs, even the fake stuff. It was one of those foods that they'd somehow managed to replicate and genetically modify without losing the flavor. Some of the kids had doused theirs with ketchup and mustard, but not me. I always ate them plain, no matter what. I took another bite, letting the synthetic yellow egg melt in my mouth, and smiled. This was even better.

I finished my meal and set it to the side, then sat there

for a while, just enjoying the quiet. No sassy nuns, no noisy kids, no Freddie pestering me with questions. Only the gentle quiet of a mostly empty megastructure, spiraling through a slip tunnel.

Before I could relish in the thought for much longer, I heard the pitter-patter of tiny feet running through the nearby hallway. I glanced up at the open door, only to see little Lex shuffling into the cafeteria. "Mr. Hughes?" she asked me. "What are you doing here? How come you're not asleep?"

"I could ask you the same thing, kid."

She gave me a mischievous grin, one that told me she was clearly up to no good. "I was just exploring." She walked over to the other side of the bench, throwing her feet over it and dangling them.

"It's a bit early for you to be exploring, don't you think?"

"I couldn't sleep. I don't know why," she said.

I gave the kid a slight nod. "I know how you feel. I've been there." I thought about my own insomnia, back in juvie. The other kids and I used to stay up late, telling stories about where we'd been before we got there. Most of the time, they were all just made up, make-believe little tales we told to impress the others, and we all knew it. None of us came from an exciting life. None of us had ever left the planet. Personally, I used to say that I was the son of a Renegade, and that somewhere out there my dad was flying around, kicking ass and getting rich; that someday he'd come back for me, and we'd do it all together. Part of me wanted to believe, but the other part knew the hard truth of it. Some nights I stayed awake thinking about the old man, wondering where he was and what he was doing. It was nights like those when I thought too much about it, the possibilities of what might have happened to him, where he might have gone. It kept my mind from winding down.

All that worry fades when you get older, and it stops happening every time you shut your eyes, but everyone still has nights like that. They just happen less often than they used to. For me, I poured myself a glass and the problem took care of itself. Too bad for Lex, because I wasn't about to give her any booze. "Do you go exploring every night?" I finally asked.

"Yeah, almost," she said, grinning.

I laughed. This whole time I'd been passed out, thinking this kid was fast asleep, but all the while, she was out and about, wandering all over this giant-ass ship. "What areas have you been going to?" I asked, genuinely curious.

"Um, I like to go to the 12th deck mostly," she said, tapping her chin and appearing to think about it. "It's pretty there."

"Pretty, huh?" I got out from the table, back on my feet. "What say we check it out and you show me?"

She swiveled around and leapt off the bench, quickly running to the hall. I could see the excitement in her face, swelling her cheeks. "Let's go! Let's go!" she exclaimed.

I eased myself up and joined her. She was suddenly so full of energy, like a switch had gone off. "Yeah, yeah, settle down, kid," I said, patting her on the head. "Don't make me regret this."

THE 12ᵀᴴ DECK was unlike any of the other places on *Titan* that I had seen before now. There was so much more machinery here. Circuitry along the walls, chairs and consoles in every spare corner, and the further we walked, the more elaborate the architecture seemed to become.

After a time, we came to a door, sealed like the one in the engine room. Just like that, Lex activated it and it opened with ease. We entered inside and continued walking deeper and deeper. For a while, it was just one hallway after the next with a few offshoots and open doors leading to nothing in particular. At least, from what I could see. I tried to stop once or twice, but Lex insisted we continue forward. Whatever we were here to see was still ahead of us.

The ceiling opened up a short time later. It was nearly twice the height of the other decks, which made me feel like a dwarf. Inside each of the rooms, I could see body-sized pods, similar but different to the ones in the medical bay. I wanted to stop and examine them, but Lex kept tugging my hand to keep going, so I let her, and we did.

Directly ahead of us, in the main atrium of what must be the central hub of whatever this was, I saw a large wall-sized machine, radiating with the blue glow. Lights seem to pulse, almost like a beating heart, but far slower. "What the hell is this thing?"

Lex giggled, letting go of my hand and running up close to the structure. As she did, her tattoos began to glow the same as the wall. I don't mean that they glowed steadily like they normally did. I mean that their glow matched the other's rhythm, coming and going with the same sort of cadence that the wall seemed to have. I didn't understand it, but something told me this was normal.

Normal for Lex, that is.

"Isn't it neat?" asked Lex. "I don't know why, but I really like it."

"But what is this thing?" I asked.

She seemed to think for a minute then shook her head. "It's just pretty. Isn't that okay? To just be pretty sometimes?"

I stared up at the wall, examining it for longer than I could say. I must've stared for several minutes, almost getting lost in the light. There were several cracks in the material, where it seemed to get brighter.

I glanced down at Lex, hoping she'd say something else to give me a clue as to what this was, what *any* of this was, but she never did. She only stood there, staring at the glow, enjoying the moment, or as she'd put it, the beauty of it all.

Part of me wanted to agree with her, that maybe sometimes being beautiful was reason enough for a thing to exist, but I'd never been such a romantic.

This structure had been *built*, created with hands like mine, and that meant it had a function. A *purpose*.

Everything artificial *always* had a purpose.

I left the wall, noticing that there were several open doorways surrounding the atrium. I walked over to one and peered inside, spotting more of those strange pods. They were larger than the medical ones, about twice the size, and uglier, like these had been thrown together without concern for aesthetics.

I walked into the room, going over to one of the pods to get a better look. They were all closed, sealed like the others we found in the medical bay. All but one, I noticed, which I hadn't spotted until just now. It stood alone, almost isolated, on the other side of the room, its lid cracked to reveal a small bed inside. It was so much smaller than the others, and thinner too.

"I see you've found the hatchery," said a familiar disembodied voice.

I turned to see Athena appear directly behind me. She gave me a pleasant smile, the way a parent does when the child does something right. I wasn't sure if it was nice or insulting.

"You know, Captain, if you were curious about this section of the ship, you could have inquired with me about it. I would've been more than happy to tell you about it or explain its function," she told me.

I cocked my brow and glanced back at the pods, then at the glowing wall where Lex was still standing. "Honestly, before I got here, I had no clue where I was heading. Once I was here, the thought to ask you just never hit me."

"I see you're interested in the graphing pods," she said.

"Graphing pods?" I asked.

She nodded. "That is the name of those machines in each of these rooms. I could see by the look on your face that you were curious about them."

I glanced at the wall again. "I'm curious about a lot of things on this deck. For example, what the hell is that thing, and why is it glowing? Also, why the hell is Lex glowing with it?"

Lex looked at me, probably hearing her own name, and waved, a big smile across her cheeks.

Athena glanced at the girl and back at me. "That is simply the power converter, which takes energy from the core and prepares it to be used in a very specific way that is unlike any other throughout this vessel."

"I take it the wall has something to do with these pods here," I asked, thumbing behind me at the room. "What are they for, exactly?"

"You are correct, Captain," she told me. "These pods draw a special kind of energy from the converters you see there. This is actually something that I have been meaning to discuss with you since your arrival. However, due to the lack of a usable core, the energy output required would have been too great for me to demonstrate the function of this section."

"And what exactly is the function, as you keep saying?" I asked.

She walked closer to where I was standing, next to the little pod, and glanced down at it. "You came here in search of something," she said. "You came here because you found a little girl who was unlike any you'd ever seen before. A little girl with answers to questions you never thought to ask."

My eyes drifted down to the infant-sized pod before me. The soft cushion was finely shaped to fit a baby's head and torso.

"Haven't you ever wondered where she came from?" asked Athena. "Since you arrived here, had it not occurred to you that perhaps you had found her birthplace already?"

I hesitated to respond. What Athena was proposing seemed impossible, that Lex could have come all that way to wind up on a backwater planet on the other side of Union space. It was a preposterous claim, wasn't it? But where else could she have come from? Where else in all the galaxy had there been people who looked like her, with tattoos that glowed blue when you touched an ancient device? Even if people from thousands of years ago had looked like that, wouldn't they all be dead by now? Wouldn't I have seen more of them, whether on the news or on the net? In the short time I had known Lex, I thought she'd been unique. A fluke accident, created or born by some harebrained scientists in a lab on some planet, probably not far from where the Union had found her. The idea that it all started here, the way Athena was proposing, halfway across the galaxy...it just seemed impossible.

Yet I believed every word of it, despite the lunacy of it all, because I'd seen enough by now to know that anything was possible.

Megastructure moons, ancient Cognitives, a lost civilization from pre-history. If so many impossible things could be true, why not this as well?

Especially now that I was standing in a room filled with ancient pods, near a glowing wall with a glowing child, talking to a woman made of light.

What was one more *impossible* thing to add to the pile?

I looked at Athena, at her calm blue eyes, and finally said, "Tell me everything."

16

"A VERY LONG TIME AGO, before humanity had ventured so far out into the stars, its primary focus was on its own refinement.

"The evolution happened faster than you might assume. A geneticist by the name of Dr. Sheldon Kane, along with his wife, Dr. Sandra Quintell, a nanoroboticist, developed a revolutionary new method to repair and maintain the immune system in such a way that it became increasingly impossible to take ill.

"The process involved a new type of nanobot technology, previously thought impossible. However, Dr. Quintell and Dr. Kane had been working on the technology in secret at their home lab for nearly 15 years. They did this, as they had said, to save their son, a cancer patient by the name of Joseph.

"When the husband and wife revealed their research to the world, it was their son who acted as living proof of their success. In a matter of days, the nanotechnology had swept through his blood stream, refined his immune system, and changed his very DNA. The public was astonished by this new revolution and its potential effects on not only medicine, but all aspects of human life.

"Suddenly, anything was possible. If this technology could be used to alter DNA, why not use it to change a person's physical appearance as well? Eye and hair color, body proportions...everything could now be custom-tailored to fit a person's ideal self.

"People had always been obsessed with how they looked, but now they really could be anyone, and now it actually would be *more* than skin deep. It would be *real* change.

"Of course, scientists the world over had taken interest in these findings, and not just for cosmetic purposes. These groups saw the research's true potential...that it could lead to a new stage in human evolution, one that no one had previously believed possible.

"A lab under the control of Monolith Industries, a for-profit research company, began development on what would eventually become known as the Immortality Project. As its name implied, the project's goal was to use nanotechnology to slow and eventually stop the aging process.

"It took nearly a decade, but their work was ultimately a resounding success. Within a few short years, Monolith Industries had developed a method to quadruple the average person's life. Eventually, that number had increased even further.

"It didn't take long for the company to begin the rollout of their new product, known as Forever Young. Right away, the product was nearly inaccessible to the average person. It was so expensive that only the richest individuals could afford to buy it, and buy it they did.

"A new class of people arose, whose entire distinction was that they never grew old and they never got sick. These became known throughout society as Eternals, while the lower class—individuals who lived only a few hundred years—were known as Transients.

"After a time, anomalies began to appear. Small changes to a person's physical appearance, largely unnoticed until it became widespread.

"The mutation didn't happen right away, but over the course of a few centuries. Certain children—those descended from other Eternals—were born with unique traits that were very much unlike their parents and ancestors. White hair, deep blue eyes, and snow-white skin. More importantly, these individuals seemed to possess an innate form of immortality, meaning they no longer required the Forever Young supplement. At long last, the next true stage of human evolution had arisen.

"As the years passed, the descendants of the Eternals, these albino offspring, became the new vanguard of the future. Presidents, governors, senators, scientists, lawyers, judges, corporate owners—all of them, Eternals.

"And because the rich and powerful never aged, because they never died, that meant that upward mobility came to a near standstill. The dream of prosperity, of pulling oneself up became nothing more than a distant dream.

"Nearly two centuries after the discovery of Forever Young, the people had had enough. The Transients rebelled against the powerful Eternals, demanding a return to the old ways. They called for opportunity, for the chance to achieve whatever they desired. There was a need in them, you see, to reach beyond themselves...beyond the borders of their stations.

"A deal was struck between the Eternals and those in charge of the rebellion. Several habitable worlds had been discovered in remote systems many light years away from Earth. The Eternals would fashion several colony ships, each one large enough to carry all who wanted to start anew. Colonization efforts had already taken place across the solar system, including Luna, Mars, and Europa, and there had been two successful missions to explore planets beyond Sol's system. However, this would be the single greatest colonization effort ever attempted, which meant it would require time and focus. Over a century, in fact.

"The Eternals and Transients worked tirelessly to make this shared dream a reality. Humanity entered a new age of shared optimism and ambition that was unlike any before it. For the first time in centuries, the masses believed their future was one of prosperity. They believed they had a chance at a better life.

"Eventually, multiple ships had been created, each with its own cognitive intelligence to guide the colonists to their respective worlds. In total, twelve seed colony ships were dispatched to various star systems throughout the galaxy. *Titan* was one such vessel, the final addition in what would ultimately amount to the largest mass exodus ever recorded.

"Most of the passengers were Transients, possessing an average unassisted lifespan of one hundred years, with a few Eternals who had volunteered to come along and assist them.

"Over the next century, the twelve colony ships expanded into the galaxy. Many of them were lost, their signals suddenly silenced, without explanation. All but *Titan* disappeared, lost to either distance or disaster. None of us could be certain.

"In time, *Titan*'s leaders believed they were all that remained of the expansion effort, and when our tritium core failed, they suspected the same fate had befallen the other colonies.

"While my colonists left and expanded to nearby habitable worlds, I watched and waited, listening for any signs of life from across the galaxy, always hoping for a response, but there was only silence, no matter where I searched.

"It was not until a few centuries ago that the silence finally broke...and I received the message that would change everything.

"'Earth has been restored,' the transmission said. 'Initiate Project Reclamation. All vessels, proceed to Earth at once.'"

I LISTENED to the Cognitive tell me the story of my ancestors, all my attention on her as the tale unfolded. When she had finally finished, I had too many questions and no idea how to ask them.

We stood there for a few minutes, silence all around us as I tried to work through the revelations I had just heard.

When I had finally processed most of what she'd told me, I decided I knew what to start with. "Did you create Lex?" I finally asked. After all that talk about Earth and starships, about genetically modified humans and nanobot technology, my first thought was of the girl.

Athena smiled. "No, I did not create her, although I did awaken her."

"If you didn't make her, who did?" I asked.

Athena frowned. "She was birthed naturally by two Eternals, but they were both killed." She paused. "Let me restate. They were *murdered* by a dissident Transient who was holding to a particularly dangerous ideology. The mother had only given birth a few months prior to her death. Shortly thereafter, the third and final Eternal to join this voyage was also killed."

"They died when she was just an infant?" I asked, glancing back at Lex. She was now curled in a ball on the floor, lying next to the wall, both of them still glowing together.

"Indeed," said the Cognitive. "The child was hidden away, here in the Hatchery, placed in cryo-sleep and left to her dreams. The Transients never woke her, eventually deciding to abandon the child to my care. It was here she remained until I awoke her."

I leaned closer to the ancient woman, my voice little more than a whisper. I didn't want the kid to hear me, not if I could help it. "And why is that, exactly? Why'd you wake her up and send her across Union space to some backwater world?"

"I wanted to lead the rest of you home," she answered. "I had tried sending messages, but I never received a response, not in all ten thousand attempts. I believe this to be a result of how far the colonist had traveled. It was not until your ship drew closer to *Titan* that I was able to open a channel, largely thanks to the turn-key you unknowingly carried with you."

"So you couldn't reach anyone because you were too far away from the rest of humanity," I said.

"Correct," said the Cognitive. "Additionally, the failing

power supply on *Titan* made it difficult to care for the child. The decision was not an easy one, but I believed it to be the optimal solution. The child, along with a data drive of information, was sent to one of the original colony locations, where over one hundred thousand of my former passengers set out to live on. Statistically, I believed it would give her the best possible chance of survival, while also allowing me to contact the descendants of my former passengers."

I remembered what I knew about where Lex had been found. It was a world called Kaldona, largely made up of farmers and fishermen. On first glance, there wasn't much to it, but the planet was well known for its ruins and history, highly regarded as one of the oldest worlds in the Union. Scholars and scientists came from all over to visit and study, which was part of how Lex had come under the control of Union scientists in the first place. They'd gone there to study, only to find a little girl with secrets of her own. Unfortunately, from what I remembered reading on the galnet, most of the original buildings and technology had been destroyed in a weather disaster nearly fifteen hundred years ago. Hardly the world Athena seemed to think it was. "You said you did this because you finally heard a transmission?" I asked.

She nodded. "Yes, Captain. For the first time in nearly two thousand years. 'Initiate Project Reclamation.'"

"What the hell does that mean?" I asked.

"That," she said, "is a question that I have been asking

myself for nearly two centuries, Captain, and it is one I wish to answer very soon."

"How's that?" I asked.

"By doing what you came here to do," she said. "By finally returning to Earth, the place where all of this first began."

17

THE NEXT MORNING, I awoke in my quarters, my thoughts still on the night before. I still couldn't believe the story Athena had told me. It felt so surreal, like a daydream you fantasized about but never expected to be real. How could it be? It was so impossible, so incredibly unbelievable, that it went beyond anything I thought I could imagine.

Maybe I just didn't want to believe it. Maybe I wanted things to be simple again, the way they used to be, back before there were Cognitives and megastructure moons. Hell, maybe I was still in shock from nearly getting my ass killed off by a squad of union strike ships. It was hard to say.

In any case, the mission was clear. Get as far away from the government as possible, stay on course, protect my crew, and find Earth. That was a simple plan. That was something I could do.

All this other bullshit was just extra, nothing that truly mattered. If it couldn't keep me and my people alive and safe, if it couldn't keep me flying, then it didn't really matter. I smirked, wondering what Hitchens might say to that. *This is all so fascinating,* he might bellow out in that voice of his. *Such a remarkable discovery. Oh, my!*

Hell, maybe I'd tell the cheeky bastard about all this later, once things had settled down. Not today, though. Not when we were in the middle of survival.

I stayed in bed for nearly an hour drifting in and out of sleep, before a voice finally forced me to get up. It was Sigmond. "Captain, your guest is requesting your presence in her quarters."

I let out a small groan at the thought of talking to that Union scientist. It was just about the last thing I felt like doing right now. "Did she say what she wanted?" I asked.

"She mentioned you telling her during your last conversation that you would let her depart sometime soon," answered the A.I.

"Oh, right. I forgot about that. Guess I'd better tell her it's gonna be a while," I said.

I climbed out of bed and threw on a shirt, and did a quick job of fixing myself up, just so I didn't look like a total shipwreck.

Alphonse was in the lounge when I left my room, much to my surprise. He was on the couch, watching the gal-net news summary for the previous day. I was about to ask him why he was on my ship, when he turned to look at me and smiled. "Ah, Captain," he said, standing to greet me. "I thought that sounded like you."

I cocked my brow. "Sounded like me?" I asked. "Do I have a bell around my neck?"

He laughed. "Where are you off to? I can tell by your pace that you're in a hurry."

"My pace, huh? Those are some good ears you've got on you, Constable," I said, walking closer to him.

"I apologize. It's the training, you see. The Constables learn to use their senses, to always be aware of their surroundings. It makes us good at our jobs."

"Not that good, considering what happened on Priscilla," I said.

He nodded. "You have a point, Captain. I suppose even the best training can't dodge bullets."

A sudden thought occurred to me. "Say, you abandoned the Union, right?"

He paused. "I don't know if that's how I would word it," he said.

"Oh? Then how would you say it?"

He tapped his chin. "I suppose I might call it a refusal of orders one knows to be unlawful."

"In that case, you think you can come with me and explain that to our new friend?" I asked.

"Are you referring to Doctor Dressler?" he asked.

"That's the one," I answered, motioning down the other hall to the doctor's room.

He nodded. "I'd be happy to help, Captain. Perhaps we can talk some sense into her."

Alphonse and I continued through the ship towards Dressler's room. Before I opened the door, I gave the Constable a brief explanation of my last conversation with the doctor. "I told her I'd give her a shuttle," I said right when we approached her door. "I still plan on it, if that's what she wants, but I was hoping you could give her your perspective. Whatever that happens to be."

He nodded. "I'd be more than happy to," he told me, facing the door.

I unlocked it, and we entered together. Dressler stood near the other side of the room with her hands on her hips, like she'd been waiting impatiently this whole time.

Her eyes widened when she saw Alphonse. I could tell she hadn't expected him to join us.

"Doc," I said, stepping into the room along with the Constable and shutting the door. "Nice to see you. Sorry to keep you waiting in here."

"Waiting?" she asked. "I've been sitting in this room for over a day, with nothing but a pad of—" She reached over to the nearby desk and grabbed the small pad, waving it around. "—of erotic fiction to read. Do you think this is some kind of joke?"

Alphonse and I exchanged a quick look. He walked

over to her and took the pad. "I'm so sorry, Doctor. That was meant for someone else," he said, blushing.

"Who in the galaxy would read such drivel?" she asked, disgusted.

"It was a gift for Al, here," I said, nodding at the Constable.

"A gift?" she asked. "What sort of person gives such a thing?"

"I believe it was meant as a prank," said Alphonse, tucking the pad behind his belt.

I snickered. "Saving that for later, Alphonse?"

He gasped, embarrassed, and took the pad out and handed it to me. "No, of course not. Here, please discard it at your leisure."

I leaned in closer to him, whispering, "I'll be sure to give this back once we're gone." I winked then turned back to Dressler. "Anyway, Doc, here's the story. I'm sorry you had to stay in here all night, but we've been kinda busy trying not to die."

She pulled her head back. "I noticed," she remarked. "I might be stuck in this room, but with all this turbulence, I assumed you had us caught up in something."

"That's right. The Union's been chasing us and I've been trying to keep my crew alive as best I can, and incidentally, that includes you. We've got an army after us."

"Did you expect otherwise when you invaded a military research facility? Of course, the Union isn't going to simply let you walk away."

"Even still, my point is that we've been preoccupied," I said. "Hell, I nearly died a little while ago. Not that I'm complaining or anything, but cut me some slack."

"Some slack?" she asked like I'd just offended her. "You've kidnapped me and stuck me in a prison cell. Excuse me if I'm less than understanding of your situation, sir."

I glanced at Alphonse. "She called me, 'sir.' Did you hear that?"

"I did," he said, holding his chin and nodding thoughtfully. "It's very respectful."

"I feel so honored," I said, holding a hand to my chest.

"If you two are finished mocking me, I'd like to discuss that shuttle you promised," said Dressler. "I want you to send me on my way."

"Can't," I said flatly. "Not right now. You'll have to wait."

"Why? Because you have people after you? Just stop the ship for two minutes and let me leave. I don't care where you do it."

"I care," I countered. "If we wait around, even for a few minutes, that's time the Union has to catch up to us, and I can't let that happen. We're on the run. Don't you get that?"

She growled in frustration, turning away from me and balling both her hands into fists. "This is ridiculous!"

I looked at Alphonse. "You talk to her."

He nodded. "I'll do what I can, but you must remember, Captain, she believes you to be nothing more than a simple brigand."

"A what?" I asked.

"You don't know what a brigand is?" he asked.

I stared at him for a long moment. "No."

He tilted his head. "It's a villain," he finally answered. "A lawbreaker. An outlaw."

"Outlaw?" I asked, glancing at the doctor. "Now that's one thing we can all agree on."

Alphonse edged his way closer to Dressler, who was still facing away from both of us. "Doctor, if you don't mind," said the Constable.

"What is it?" she asked furiously. "Come to tell me why you betrayed your own government?"

Her words didn't seem to faze him. "I can see you're tired and agitated. I had to wait in a room like this one for several days before you met me. I understand how you must be feeling."

"Do you? Because you don't seem very angry about it. They captured you and made you a prisoner, so the first thing you do is join them?" she asked. "What's wrong with you, Constable?"

"A great many things, I'm sure the Red Tower will say," he told her. "Nonetheless, Captain Hughes did not capture me."

"Hey," I said. "Sure I did."

Alphonse ignored me. "I let myself be taken, because I

learned a dark truth and wanted to verify it. I became a prisoner so that I might understand."

"You let them take you?" she asked.

He nodded. "I had several chances to run," he explained. "Even after I was in a cell, I could have fled and gotten free. I chose to remain with these people, to watch them with my own eyes."

"Why in the galaxy would you do such a thing?" she asked.

He paused, rubbing the side of his chin. "Have you heard of the Old Earth theory?" he finally asked. "Surely, since you worked on Priscilla, you must know of it."

"Of course I do," she said.

"What have you heard?" he asked.

"I'm not telling you. I swore an oath of confidence. The research is classified. All I can say is that I know about the theory," she said.

"Let me help you," continued Alphonse. "The Old Earth Theory states that all human life shares a single common origin point—that being Earth. This is very different from the fairytale that parents tell their children, which describes Earth as a fantasy world of magic and dragons." The Constable cleared his throat. "Instead, the Old Earth Theory outright denies any such story in favor of a more realistic approach, based entirely on evidence collected by the Union. According to such evidence, researchers conclude that Earth was once a thriving paradise of technological wonder. Its people were said to have conquered disease, invented the first slipspace drives, and mastered many other fields of study."

Hearing Alphonse talking about Earth reminded me of the conversation I had with Athena the previous night in the Hatchery. Everything she had told me had seemed so impossible. Now Alphonse was saying the same things, although with less detail than Athena had.

Still, the overlap surprised me. The Union knew more than I thought about Earth, which only meant they had even more of a reason to keep pursuing us.

"What does any of that matter?" asked the doctor. "You're talking about things that have nothing to do with either of us."

"Ah," said Alphonse. "But that is where you are mistaken, Doctor."

Alphonse looked at me, almost like he wanted my permission. I responded with a short nod, giving him the all-clear.

He continued. "The Union is seeking to rediscover Earth, and in doing so, it has expanded its research efforts throughout the galaxy. It has invaded neutral zones on all sides of its borders, slaughtered countless people on dozens of worlds, and abducted hundreds of children to perform experiments on."

"Experiments?" asked Dressler. "Are you referring to the Blue Ink Experiment?"

Alphonse smiled. "Very good, Doctor."

She thought for a moment then shook her head. "No,

that's not right. Those experiments ended from lack of progress."

"Incorrect," said Alphonse. "They ended because the lab lost its control subject."

"Control subject?" she repeated.

He nodded. "The experiments revolved around replicating a certain tattoo on each of the children, which would—"

"Which would give them the ability to control Origin Tech," finished Dressler. "I know."

"What you might not be aware of is that the tattoos were based on an original source. Another child who presented the marks at birth, or so it was theorized. No one knew for certain, since no one knew where the child had originated," explained Alphonse.

Dressler scoffed. "Are you suggesting that the researchers were only trying to replicate an existing tattoo from another child?"

"Indeed, I am, Doctor, and I mean to tell you that the only reason the trials ended was because the child went missing." He paused. "Well, she was kidnapped, in point of fact."

"Kidnapped?" asked Dressler. "That can't be true. None of it was in the files I read. How have I not heard of this?"

"Because the details of this child are highly classified, beyond the typical blue clearance level," he said.

She listened to every word he told her, taking it all in,

then let out a short sigh and shook her head. "This is all fascinating, Constable, but I have to say, I don't know what the point of any of it is. What does the Old Earth Theory or the Blue Ink Experiment have to do with you, me, or that Renegade behind you?"

"Everything," I finally said, taking a step closer to the two of them. "That child he's been telling you about is here. Her name is Lex. She was rescued from a lab to save her life, and I'll be damned if I'll let the Union take her back."

Dressler's mouth dropped. "She's here...?"

Alphonse nodded. "Correct, and now I hope you understand my role in all of this, Doctor. I came here because I wanted to know whether the child was real and worth protecting. I wanted to see the Renegade responsible for her safety and decide for myself."

"Decide what?" asked Dressler.

"Whether I could trust him enough to join him," Alphonse said, looking back at me. "Whether he was everything they said he was...or something else altogether."

I WAS SITTING in the *Star* when I got the call. "Jace, get your ass to the bridge. We need you up here," said Abigail.

The com cut out before I could answer. "That was rather abrupt," said Sigmond.

"I think she might still be pissed at me," I said, sitting on my sofa with my feet on the table.

"In fairness, sir, you did force both of us to abandon you, despite our protests," argued Siggy.

"What can I say, Siggy? Sometimes I like to go at it alone," I said with a grin.

I made my way out of the ship and headed towards *Titan's* bridge. When I got there, I found Abigail, Freddie, Hitchens, Octavia, and Alphonse all standing there, watching the screen on the wall. They all turned to me the moment I entered, but I could already see what the problem was before anyone had the chance to speak.

The monitor behind them showed an image that I quickly recognized. It was Gen. Brigham's flagship itself, the *Galactic Dawn*, flying straight through a slip tunnel. Green walls of lightning surrounded it, reflecting emerald light on its hull. The effect made the ship look almost angry.

I stepped into the bridge, letting the door slide shut behind me. "Looks like we have a problem," I said.

Freddie scratched his head. "You could say that," he said, glancing back at the screen.

"Is that what I think it is?" I asked, walking closer.

"It seems the enemy refuses to quit," said Alphonse.

"The enemy?" I asked, cocking my brow at him.

He smiled. "I think I've made it clear which side I'm on, Captain."

I glanced at Abigail. "Is it just the one ship?"

"In the tunnel behind us?" she asked. "Yes. Elsewhere? Hard to say."

Athena materialized in front of us. "Welcome, Captain Hughes. To answer your question…" She waved her hand, changing the screen.

I saw another ship, this one much smaller, with the Sarkonian design on it. Before I could say anything, the screen changed again to show another Union ship. A second later, it changed to another, and then another. In seconds, the screen switched dozens of times, cycling through a list of enemy ships, almost overwhelming me with how fast they were coming.

"Holy shit," I muttered, blinking at the fluttering display. "Are you saying that we have a small armada coming our way?"

"It's worse than that," said Abigail.

"How can it be worse than that?" I asked.

Athena answered me this time. "Each of the ships is pursuing us from a different direction, across multiple tunnels. The tunnel we are now traveling through already has an endpoint, which means they already know where we will arrive."

"I thought you could form tunnels with *Titan* and go wherever you want," I said.

"That is true," said Athena. "However, while I did form a new slip tunnel, we returned to retrieve you soon afterwards."

"And?" I asked.

Octavia smacked the side of my arm. "After we picked you up, there wasn't enough time for her to make a brand-new tunnel. She had to use the existing one."

Abigail nodded. "The same one we were on our way to take before you tried to defuse that mine and then take on those soldiers all by yourself." She glared at me. "Like an idiot."

I ignored her and looked at the Cognitive. "Isn't there a way for you to change directions?"

Athena frowned. "I can break an existing tunnel, but I cannot change course midflight. Its direction is fixed."

Freddie raised a finger. "So why can't we just break out of the tunnel and form a brand-new one?"

"Because that scenario comes with its own set of problems, given where we might arrive," said Athena. She turned around and waved her hand at the screen. The display changed to show a planet that I instantly recognized. It was a place that I'd made a point of avoiding, and for good reason.

"Isn't that...?" asked Abigail.

"Maelstrom," said Alphonse. "One of the strongest military outposts in the entire Union. It's also home to the Constables."

"That's where the Constables live?" asked Freddie.

"Where they convene," said Alphonse. "Only a few live there. For the most part, it's a heavily guarded military instillation. Typically, there are less than one hundred

Constables on site. The rest are either at the Red Tower or on their own missions."

I shook my head. "We can't stop there. We'll keep going until we reach a better spot."

"This tunnel's path leads even further into Union territory," said Athena. "The next location is Androsia itself."

"The *capital?*" I asked, spitting out the word like it was toxic. "Are you kidding me?"

"I'm afraid not," said the Cognitive.

"You heard her, Jace," said Abigail. "We can either follow this tunnel to its end, get out near Maelstrom, or the point between, which would be—"

"Near the Androsia system," I finished. "Yeah, I got it."

I stared at the planet, letting the air around me fill with a long silence. No matter which option I chose, the *Galactic Dawn* would still follow us. It had set itself along the same path as us, which meant that no matter what I decided, the end result would still be a showdown. "How big are the numbers at Maelstrom?" I finally asked.

The Cognitive zoomed the image of the planet in, showing a small group of ships. "Currently, enemy forces in this region are reduced."

"That's because they don't know we can rip a tunnel open and surprise them," said Freddie.

"You're actually correct," said Alphonse. He crossed his arms. "The Union has every ship in the area heading to the endpoint of this tunnel. They'll converge on that location and try to surprise us."

"Which means," I said, narrowing my eyes at the planet. "All we have to do is drop out at Maelstrom long enough to rip another hole in the sky."

"Sounds about right," said Octavia.

I nodded. "How long before we arrive?"

"Up to fifteen hours," said Athena. "Approximately."

"Up to?" I echoed.

The Cognitive nodded. "I have slowed our movement to allow us more time. If need be, I can also bring us to a full stop inside the tunnel."

"No, we're not hiding out in this tunnel," I said.

"Is fifteen hours enough time to get prepared?" asked Freddie.

"It will be," I responded. "We'll make sure we're ready."

"But even with *Titan* and the *Renegade Star*, we barely had enough firepower for the last fight," said Octavia.

She was right. *Titan* still didn't have full access to its weapons . I also had no idea how many hits its shield could take before collapsing.

"Actually, Captain, now that *Titan*'s systems have partially been restored, there is one thing that we can do to better our odds of survival," said Athena. "Do you recall the ship you arrived in originally?"

"You mean the little triangular one?" I asked, thinking back to a few days ago, when we visited the ruins on that planet, the same day we discovered the truth about this moon. It felt like a lifetime ago. "What about it?"

"Those ships contain their own weapons systems. Before now, they were inoperable, due to *Titan's* power deficiency," she explained. "However, I believe that now they may prove functional, should you see fit to use them."

"You're telling me we've got other ships we can use to fight with?" I asked, surprised she hadn't brought this up before.

"There is only one caveat," she said.

"Caveat?" I repeated, glancing at Abigail.

"There's a catch," the nun explained.

"Oh. What is it?"

The Cognitive took a step closer to me, raising her finger and touching the blue mark on her neck. "You will need to receive your key."

18

I WAS INSIDE THE POD, my arms at my sides. There was more than enough room for me, but I still felt claustrophobic. You would think for somebody who had spent half his life on a spaceship, I wouldn't mind feeling a bit cramped from time to time, but maybe the small space wasn't the problem.

Maybe I just didn't want a bunch of needles drilling into my skin.

Yeah, that was probably it.

I had asked Athena if the rest of the crew could undergo this treatment, but unfortunately, as she put it, there wasn't enough time to synthesize the necessary compounds required to make the marks. There was only enough for one person, since the core had only been online for a short while. Because of time constraints and because I refused to let one of my crew take a risk that I wasn't willing to take myself, I volunteered to be the guinea pig. If Athena could manage another batch of whatever the hell this treatment was before Brigham's ship showed up, Abigail, Freddie, and Bolin had already offered themselves as potential candidates.

But all of that hinged on whether or not the first attempt was a success.

Here goes nothing, I thought.

"Don't worry, Captain," said Athena. "The process should be relatively painless. You will experience a strange tingling sensation, followed by something akin to swimming in a cool stream of flowing water."

I stared up at the Cognitive. "I don't give two damns what it feels like," I said frankly. "It has to be done, so let's get on with it."

I hated it when people tried to make you feel better about something you had to do. Nothing they could ever say was going to prevent it from happening, so why not just get the hell on with it?

Athena gave me a comforting smile and backed away, letting the pod hatch close on top of me. I watched while the machine sealed itself, trapping me inside, then waited for the next step in the process to begin.

It didn't take very long. Strange gas began to enter the pod. It smelled like potatoes, oddly enough, or maybe it was plastic. Before I could argue with myself any further, I felt a small prick in my left shoulder. I turned my head and saw a glowing needle of hard light, injecting a blue liquid into my arm.

The pain was brief, like a small pinch. A second later, I felt a strange coolness beginning in my shoulder and moving along my arm. Before I could react, I felt another prick, this time in my back like before, and a soft and almost pleasant coolness followed. Another prick on my lower back, and then my side, and then my other shoulder. I felt all of them at once, a dozen across half my body and all of them happening within a few seconds.

And as fast as they happened, it was all suddenly over. The cool rush of the blue liquid crawled smoothly through my bloodstream, filling me with calmness, like I was in a pool of flowing water.

I began to think I might grow tired, sleepy from the effects, but it never happened. Instead, I only grew more awake as I saw the illumination beneath my skin. It glowed faintly at first but slowly built. After only a few moments, the light was stronger and more prevalent than before.

The blue glow moved, forming a pattern on my skin, creating an intricate design that I instantly recognized, because I'd seen it so many times before. It was the same design that Lex had. The same symbols that were on Athena. Somehow, because of this pod, I was beginning to look like them.

The process only took a few more moments, as the cool blue liquid continued to move throughout my body, creating more tattoos. Eventually, the glowing lights stopped radiating and the cool sensation I had felt finally dissipated, returning to normal.

The hatch cracked open, and I leaned forward out of the pod, pushing myself onto my feet.

Athena approached me, a curious expression on her face. "How do you feel, Captain?"

I glanced to my side, examining my arms and noticing the tattoos. They looked tribal, almost, and somehow formal. I couldn't believe that such strange and detailed markings had been placed on me in a matter of minutes, all over my shoulders, arms, and torso. "I feel good," I said, after a few seconds. "That wasn't bad at all."

"I'm glad to hear it," said the Cognitive. "If you require time to rest, I will understand."

I ran my fingers along my tattooed skin but felt no pain or bumps. It was like they had always been there. "No," I said, looking back at her. "We need to finish preparing for what's about to come. Brigham is on his way to kill us all. There's little time to waste."

I SAT inside one of the little triangle ships, looking over the controls. They were in a foreign language, one that I couldn't read or even recognize. I knew this was the language of the ancients, because it was all over *Titan*. There wasn't enough time to actually learn it, so I'd have to simply memorize the controls as best I could. "Which button is the ignition?" I asked.

Athena's voice chimed in over my com. "There is no need for that," she told me.

"What do you mean?" I asked.

"Simply put your hand on the interface module," she said.

I examined the dash in front of me, looking for whatever the hell an interface module was supposed to be. I was about to ask for specifics, when I saw a small hand-sized panel. I reached out and touched it, expecting nothing to happen.

The newly created tattoos on my arm began to glow, surprising me. Immediately after, the panel followed suit, illuminating itself to match the color of my tattoo. "Excellent work, Captain," said Athena. "The interface is live."

"Now what?" I asked, keeping my hand on the panel.

"You must imagine your commands," she explained. "Think about the actions you wish the vessel to take."

Think about the actions, I thought. *Sounds like a bunch of bullshit, but okay. Let's go, you stupid ship. Initiate thrusters.*

Nothing happened.

"What's the deal? I thought this thing was supposed to listen to my thoughts," I said.

"Apologies, Captain. I should have been more specific," said Athena. "Try to imagine what you would like the vessel to do, but you must visualize it happening. The interface is built to understand mental images and desires above all else, but they must be focused and at the forefront of your mind."

"Visualize it, huh?" I asked.

I imagined the ship, igniting its thrusters, trying to visualize how the process might work, even though I knew absolutely nothing about the design of the ships. I imagined the little triangle lifting off the ground and—

The ship suddenly vibrated, humming steadily as its engines roared to life. Before I could react, we eased off the deck and began floating in the air nearly a meter up. The sudden reaction startled me, but in a good way, and I couldn't help but grin. "Now that's what I'm talking about," I said, smacking the side of my chair.

"Excellent work, Captain," congratulated Athena. "Try to move the ship, but only a few meters. Be very careful. We are still in slipspace, after all. You don't want to accidentally leave the landing bay."

If I hadn't known any better, I would've sworn the Cognitive was teasing me.

I imagined the ship moving, slightly to the right, visualizing the process in my mind. As I did, the vessel began to shift, tilting slightly to the right and moving. I felt a rush of excitement, a sense of satisfaction in what I was doing. It reminded me of the first time I shot a gun, back when I was seven. Later, again, when I pulled off my first heist.

Good times.

The ship jerked forward suddenly, surprising the crap out of me. I pulled my hand off the pad, causing my tattoos and the dash to both stop glowing. The ship fell smack into the deck. My chest slammed into the harness around me, nearly knocking the wind out of me. "Gods!" I snapped.

"You must focus and concentrate, Captain," informed the Cognitive.

"Are you telling me that if I don't concentrate, I'll crash the damn ship?" I asked.

"That is correct," said Athena. "But don't worry. Once you master the controls, you'll be able to fly without hesitation. It will be like second nature to you."

"And how long does that usually take?" I asked.

"The process varies between users, but you are doing well," she said. "Please, Captain, do not relent."

I growled at her for not answering my question, but let it go. I touched the dash and visualized the ship lifting off the ground, and a moment later, it did. The engines reignited and once again brought me a meter off the deck, where it began to hover in place.

I imagined moving to the left and to the right, then forward and backwards. The ship followed my every command, doing precisely as I ordered. Before I knew it, I was flying the vessel around the mostly empty landing bay, slowly maneuvering horizontally and vertically, without much of a problem. Thirty minutes into the practice run, I decided I had had enough and was ready to move on. "We don't have much time, Athena. I think you ought to show me how to use the weapons on this thing," I said.

"Please allow me a moment," said Athena. "I currently

have the weapon systems deactivated. Given your inexperience, I thought it prudent to disable them in order to avoid disaster. I will reactivate them, although they will not be lethal."

"Not lethal?" I asked, slightly confused by the statement. I couldn't imagine what that might mean.

"The weapon systems on each of the ships uses a variation of hard light technology. By disabling one of the options in the projectors, only the visual effects of the weapon will function."

"Are you saying that I can't blow anything up?" I asked.

"That is correct, Captain," she told me.

"Damn," I said, floating the ship over to the other side of the bay. "And here I was, thinking the only way to master this would be to blow a hole in something."

"Perhaps next time," said Athena.

There went that sarcasm again.

IN ONLY AN HOUR, I had the controls pretty well figured out. I could fly in any direction, perform a small number of maneuvers, and successfully navigate the weapon systems.

A few hours into it, I called the rest of my crew and told them to meet me in the conference room. Once they all showed up, Athena gave me the signal and I set the ship down and went to join the others.

Now that I had a handle on things, it would be good to regroup and discuss the next step.

I entered the conference room and decided to remain standing, while several of the others took their seats. I'd been sitting on the strike ship for a while and my ass was killing me.

"How did it go?" Asked Octavia.

"I heard you crashed one of the ships a few times," said Freddie.

I gave Freddie a threatening look. "It took me a few minutes to get a handle on the controls, but once I did, it wasn't so bad."

"Can the rest of us start?" asked Abigail.

"That's up to Athena, isn't it?" I said.

Athena had already materialized and was standing quietly off to the side, observing the meeting. She took a step forward and gave the group a kind smile. "I will have enough of the treatment ready for one more dosage in approximately eight hours."

"Aren't we arriving at around that time?" asked Freddie.

"That is correct," said the Cognitive.

I cursed under my breath. It seemed like every time we took a step forward, something else happened to create yet another barrier in our path and slow us down. We now had access to another ship, but I could barely fly it and we didn't have enough time for the others to undergo the transition. We'll have to take Brigham on with only *Titan*, the *Star*, and one of the little strike ships in our possession, despite there being literally hundreds sitting in the two dozen landing bays on this moon-sized vessel. "If this is the best we can do," I said, leaving out my own frustration, "then we'll make it work. We've been in tougher scrapes than this, and with fewer options, and we still pulled ourselves out of the fire."

Bolin raised his hand slightly, cringing a little with his shoulders. "I did lose a finger the day we met. Not that I'm complaining."

Octavia glanced up at Bolin. "Really? Come talk to me when you're in a wheelchair."

"Okay," I said. "So it wasn't all rainbows and sunshine. I get that. My point is we survived…and none of you are dead. That's gotta count for something."

"Damn right," said Abigail.

Bolin nodded. "You're right," the former merchant said. He smiled. "My daughter is alive because of you. That is a debt I can never repay."

"All of us are here because of you, Jace," said Octavia. "You, Abigail, and Lex. We are here because we believed in the cause, so we don't need a fancy speech about how tough we are or how far we've come. All we need is for you to do what you do best. Find us a way out and kill as many as you can in the process."

"Well, damn, Octavia," I said, crossing my arms. "That's a better speech than what I had planned. Straight and to the point."

She smirked. "Don't get used to it. I've never been the motivational type."

"I assume you have a plan, Captain," said Hitchens, who was standing right behind Octavia.

I gave him a nod. "Now that you mention it, Professor," I said. "I think I just might."

19

I SAT inside the little triangular strike ship, waiting for *Titan* to exit slipspace. It would only be a short while now, and then the game would begin.

"Mr. Hughes," said a soft voice, coming from the chair beside me.

I looked down at Lex, sitting there with her feet dangling above the floor. She stared up at me with curious eyes. "What's up, kid?"

She looked back down, almost hesitantly, like she didn't know how to say it...or if she should.

"You're worried," I eventually said. "Is that it?"

She nodded. "You said it's dangerous."

I'd told her the truth only an hour ago. I had thought she had a right to know what was happening around her, to the people in her life. "I did, didn't I?" I asked. "But you know me, don't you, kid? I don't go down so easy."

"Yeah," she said in a soft voice.

I could see the fear in her eyes. It was the sort of worry you get when you don't know all the angles, when you can't make the perfect prediction. It's the unknowing of it all, like the moment you see the other guy draw his gun, and you don't know if you'll be fast enough. It's that dread you have before the doctor comes in and tells you about your mother…and even though you've played the story out in your head a hundred times already, you still don't know for sure how hard the truth will hit you…because you can't.

Then Lex told me what I already knew she'd say. "I just don't want you to die."

The words turned my stomach, even more than I thought they would. Not because I hated them, but because I understood where they came from.

That fear, clawing in the back of her mind.

We were both quiet for a moment. "You're scared," I finally told her.

She nodded slowly.

I was slow to continue. I didn't know how to talk about any of this stuff, especially to a little girl. "It's okay to be scared," I muttered. "Everyone else is afraid too."

"You're not," she whispered.

"You think so?" I asked, straightening up in my seat. I cleared my throat. "I didn't know you could read my thoughts, kid."

"You're never scared, even when the bad people come," she said, looking at me. "You're always brave."

I laughed. "Funny, I thought *you* were the brave one." I shook my head. "I get scared all the time, Lex."

"R-really?" she asked, a wide-eyed expression on her face.

"Oh, yeah," I said. "Every time I go on a job. Every time I'm about to get into a fight. Lately, it seems like it happens every day. Point is, everyone gets scared. It's just a feeling you get, like instinct." I took a short breath. "But that's a good thing."

"It is?" asked Lex.

I nodded. "Fear…keeps you awake, even when you're tired. It opens your eyes…teaches you what to look out for. In some ways, fear can be your friend, if you let it."

"A friend? Really?" she asked.

"You just have to know how to listen," I said, tapping my chest. "Understand what it's trying to tell you."

"I didn't know it was talking," she said.

"Oh, yeah," I said, nodding. "There's always something, like a voice deep down inside, telling where the danger is, teaching you how to stay alive. All you gotta do is open your ears and listen."

She sat there, staring at the dash for a long while, taking in what I had told her. "So fear is good," she finally said, turning to me. "You can be scared and it's okay."

"Right," I said.

"Then we're both scared," she told me. "We just have to listen."

I nodded. "Scared like crazy," I said. "But don't tell anyone. I've got a reputation."

She giggled. "Me too! I've got a reputation!"

"You sure do, kid," I said, patting her on the head, and we both laughed.

"WHAT'S OUR STATUS, ATHENA?" I asked. The time for the mission was at hand, and I was sitting in my strike ship, hand on the dash, ready to go.

"*Titan* is currently passing through the Maelstrom system. We will arrive in empty space, less than a light-year from the planet, in approximately five minutes," she answered. "Any longer and we will be closer to Androsia."

"Everyone hear that?" I asked over the com.

"Got it," said Abigail, who was on the bridge of the *Renegade Star*, manning its controls. Much as it pained me to let someone else fly my ship, she was the only one I trusted to get the job done. "Frederick and I will be ready." She paused. "And Sigmond too, of course."

"Correct," said Sigmond. "I am at your disposal, Ms. Pryar."

"We'll get this moon to safety, Captain," said Freddie.

"Octavia?" I said, glancing across the deck from inside my little ship. "How about the rest of you?"

"We know the plan," said the former Union medic. "Alphonse is getting ready to undergo the same treatment in just a few minutes. If need be, we'll send him out."

"Are you sure about that guy?" asked Freddie. "Seems like we'll be putting a lot of trust in him in case things go wrong."

"He's the only one who can do it," said Octavia. "He has the right training, he can adapt quickly under pressure, and he has experience with flying."

"Relax, Fred. Let's just hope it doesn't get to that point," I said.

He sighed but straightened himself and nodded. "Right. We can do this."

"No doubt about that," said Abby.

Athena broke in before I could say anything else. "I will require at least twenty minutes to create a new long-range slipspace tunnel. You must do what you can until enough time has passed. You must not fail."

"I get it, lady," I muttered. "I won't screw it up." Then I added to myself, *Because if I do, I'm dead.*

"We'll head to *Titan*'s bridge while you two finish preparations," said Octavia. She turned in the wheelchair, rolling away from us. "Good luck."

Hitchens and Bolin waved, each looking strikingly similar from this distance.

I made a gun with my fingers and pretended to shoot at them, which caused Hitchens to clutch his belly and laugh. They went inside, along with Lex, who was holding Camilla's hand. Lex's eyes lingered on me for just a moment before she finally turned the corner.

I let out a short sigh and tapped the com in my ear. "We all set over there, Abby?"

"We're ready, Jace."

"Good," I said, clearing my throat. I was quiet for a moment, trying to gather my thoughts.

"Arriving at destination in 15 seconds," announced Athena.

So much for taking a moment, I thought.

I cracked my neck, spine, elbows, and knuckles. "Here goes nothing," I muttered, placing my hand on the dash control panel and visualizing my strike ship lifting off the deck floor. I felt the rumble beneath me, and suddenly, I was airborne, moving toward the landing bay entrance.

I floated there for only a moment before Athena gave me the go-ahead. "*Titan* has successfully emerged from the slip tunnel. Please proceed. Good luck, Captain," said the Cognitive.

"Thanks," I said, bringing the ship out of the landing bay and into open space. "We're sure as hell going to need it."

ACCORDING TO ATHENA, *Titan* would need several minutes to recharge its core to near completion and then create a new slip tunnel. To hasten the process, it would need to bring down its shields and avoid any unnecessary combat. Of course, if any enemy ships came close enough to pose an immediate threat, shields would be raised and *Titan* would obliterate any threats that came to it, but the longer we could go without a fight, the better.

Which was where Abigail, Freddie, and I came into the picture. It was our job to distract and slow down the few dozen small to mid-sized ships in the local systems should they attack. The *Galactic Dawn* might end up being a problem once it arrived, but we'd adjust to the situation as it developed. All we had to do was follow the plan.

"Athena," I began. "Go ahead and begin moving into position. Remember, stay in the upper atmosphere of that planet. Focus on recharging that core so we can get the hell out of here."

"Understood," said the Cognitive.

"Sir," interjected Sigmond. "I am detecting multiple incoming vessels, responding to our arrival."

"What kind of ships are we talking about here, Siggy?" I asked.

"Fifteen small to mid-size Union attack ships," informed the A.I.

I tabbed the console and mentally told it to run a quick scan of the system, just like Athena had shown me. When I did, the screen on top of the dash changed to show a readout of six planets as well as *Titan*, the *Renegade Star*, and my location.

I continued to watch the readout as *Titan* began to

move away from our present location, towards the gas giant on the edge of the solar system. Athena would wait there until the last possible moment before the *Galactic Dawn* arrived. She would need all the time she could get to charge that core, and I was going to make damn sure she had it. The more energy we could accumulate, the further away from the Union we could get.

I watched *Titan* edge its way closer to the gas giant, until it was inside the upper stratosphere.

"Core is at 54 percent capacity," informed Athena. "Beginning charging sequence."

"Enemy vessels inbound. Arrival time is two minutes and counting," informed Sigmund.

I commanded my little ship to raise its shields, and it did so instantly without me having to say a word. "Abby, you sure you're ready for this?" I asked.

"Me?" she asked, acting like the question had been a surprise. "I'd be more worried about yourself, flying that weird little ship around after you only had a few hours to train in it."

"It's easy once you get the hang of it," I told her. I imagined the ship performing a horizontal spin, and then it did, followed by a vertical roll. "See? Flies like a dream."

"No need to show off," she said.

I heard Freddie in the background laughing. "The captain sure is something, isn't he?"

"Sit down and shut up, Frederick," said Abigail. "You'll give him an even bigger ego if you keep that up."

"Pardon the interruption, everyone," said Sigmond. "Enemy ships have arrived. I thought you might want to know."

I examined the radar, spotting several dots on the other end of the system.

"You heard him," I said to everyone. "Time to go to work."

THE BLINKING RED dots edged closer with each passing second.

Abigail activated the *Renegade Star*'s cloaking device, while I brought my ship around to the back of a nearby planetoid. These ancient Earth ships didn't have cloaks— hell if I understood why—but unless you knew what you were looking for, they were nearly impossible to detect with traditional scanning equipment. The same was true of *Titan*.

If only we could've masked the slip tunnel, we might have been able to go totally undetected, but even that went beyond Athena's abilities.

No big deal, I thought, watching as the first four ships came around the edge of the nearby planet. *We'll just have to play with what we have.*

The ships passed by my position, heading to the slip tunnel we had arrived on. As they did, I pulled the strike ship around and targeted the one at the center of the pack.

I imagined my ship firing the same blue blast as before, back in the landing bay, and suddenly, it happened. The light burst out of my left wing, traveling rapidly towards the others.

With that, the shield surrounding the four ships cracked apart, dissolving in a quick second, causing the enemy fighters to disperse.

"Now, Abby!" I snapped.

The *Renegade Star* decloaked on the opposite side of the fighters and began firing a spray of rounds, followed by the quad cannons.

Before the other ships could get very far, Abby had made quick work of the first one, ripping it to shreds. The *Renegade Star*'s cannons launched a set of missiles, each one aimed at a different ship. They barely had the chance to react before the torpedoes tore through their hulls and sent them to hell.

I set my sights on the last of the four, then ordered another volley from my cannons. The hit plowed through his wing, forcing him into a spin as the metal turned to dust. Abby took the opportunity to follow it up with her own attack, raining gunfire on him. The bullets sprayed diagonally across the hull, cutting through like paper and hitting the engine. The ship exploded in seconds, signaling our success.

"Nice one!" I called.

Before she could respond, I saw the other red dots blink on my dash, telling me the fight was far from over.

"Cloak yourself!" I shouted. "We've got more company!"

The *Renegade Star* faded, blurring back into the darkness of space. I could still follow her position with my radar, which meant I'd know exactly where she was at any given moment, making it easier to maneuver these fighters around to give her an advantage. That was always the key to victory. You had to control the battlefield.

Twelve more blips made their way towards me. My best guess was that the first wave had been closer when we arrived, which was unfortunate for them. If only they had waited for the rest of their friends, they might have lasted a bit longer.

Not much longer, mind you, but a little more. I wasn't taking any prisoners today. If you threatened my ship and my crew, you were done.

The remaining 12 ships were fast approaching, their destination being the destroyed ships of their fallen friends. I couldn't imagine the confusion that must have been going through their minds at that moment.

But they would understand soon enough.

I fired a shot of blue energy directly into the last ship to arrive. It ran straight through the hull and into the cockpit, creating a hole so large you could float through it. Somehow, the vessel didn't split completely apart, but it was well on its way.

The other fighters turned toward me, firing rapidly and unloading a wide spray of bullets. The gunfire swept across my side, largely missing me before several shots struck my shield. I shook it off, returning fire with my beam cannon, targeting the nearest ship in the group.

The squad moved towards me, breaking off into two sets, each with their own shield.

The *Renegade Star* dropped its cloak and began unloading its quad cannons on one of the groups.

I decided that was my cue to take the other.

Bringing my ship forward, I dove beneath the oncoming squad. I tilted my ship back, firing a blast directly into the center of their shield. They took it, much to my surprise, and the shield remained.

I dodged enemy fire, rolling to my left and pulling up, then to the right. Several shots hit my shield but did very little damage.

This was one hell of a ship.

I sent another blast into the squad's shield, finally cracking it to pieces and destroying the centermost vessel. The beam also managed to catch the edge of one of the other ships, releasing atmosphere and sending it careening into another vessel, effectively disabling three of them at once. There were only two left in the squad, making for a quick clean up.

It was a good thing too, because there was no way Abby would be able to handle all six of those other strike ships on her own, even with Siggy and Freddie to help her. As much as I loved the *Star*, it wasn't a warship. It could only do so much against that many—

Before I could finish the thought, two of the ships in the other group exploded. The *Renegade Star* flew straight through the debris, letting the shattered bits of metal deflect off its shield. A blast exploded from the quad cannons, decimating two of the other vessels, leaving only one behind.

The final ship began to run, attempting to make its way out of the system. The *Star* let out a spray of bullets, following the ship as it made its escape, finally tagging its tail, then moved along its hull, ripping it to shreds.

I whistled. "Damn, Abby."

"You sound surprised," returned the nun over the com.

"Maybe a little," I said, snickering.

A sudden burst of green light sparked nearby, like a manifesting thunderstorm. It was the rift, the slip tunnel reopening. "Jace!" I heard Abigail shout.

"I see it," I answered. "Athena, what's the status of that core?"

"Tritium core is currently at 87 percent," said the Cognitive.

"Not quite there," I muttered, turning my ship towards the opening tunnel. I wasn't sure what we could do against a vessel as powerful as the *Galactic Dawn*, but we'd hold this position for as long as possible.

The tear opened and the carrier ship began to emerge. I could see its hull, massive as it was, with its name etched on the side in gold letters.

A voice came over the com before the carrier had fully

emerged. "This is General Brigham of the Union Fleet. Captain Hughes, respond immediately."

I was surprised to hear the old man speak, since I never accepted the call, but I quickly let it go. I didn't have Sigmond to filter the coms, I had to remind myself.

I pictured Brigham's face as he repeated the transmission. How anyone could follow me this far and still have enough fight in them was beyond me.

An image appeared on my console, depicting an older-looking man in a Union military uniform. It was Brigham, much to my surprise. "Captain Hughes, respond."

"What the hell?" I asked.

Brigham cocked his brow at the sound of my voice. "Hughes? Have you decided to turn yourself in?"

I paused, hesitating to answer. Why was he able to hear me? Had I accidentally opened the com? It must have been triggered by my subconscious. I was still getting used to controlling this ship, so maybe I'd done this accidentally.

I cleared my throat, composing myself. "General," I said with a monotone voice. "What can I do for you?"

Brigham seemed unmoved by my question. He was stone cold. "You can surrender yourself at once, Captain. Do so immediately and I will ensure your crew survives the day."

"Let's not waste time with this again," I said, thinking back to the last encounter I had with this man. He'd made the same offer and I'd promptly ignored him. "You want the kid. I'm not giving her up. That puts us at a crossroads."

"Indeed, it does," said the general. "You must understand that my capabilities far outweigh your own, though. Compare our ships, Captain. The *Galactic Dawn* is the flagship of the fleet. It has no equal."

"That's true," I said with a nod. "You're walking around strutting that beast of a ship and I'm over here with the *Renegade Star*. There ain't much of a comparison."

"I'm glad you see that," he said.

I raised a finger. "It's a good thing I'm not flying that ship, then, isn't it?"

He paused, furrowing his brow. "Excuse me?"

"You'll see," I said, swiftly ordering my ship to begin accelerating. I visualized the com shutting off, and the image of the general disappeared.

The strike ship moved toward the *Galactic Dawn*, followed by the *Star*. I unloaded my beam cannon on the first section of the *Dawn*'s hull, leaving a long drag mark across the metal plating. It looked like a burn, though I was certain it hadn't done much damage. Larger Union ships had several thick layers of plating, making it difficult to break through the hull and cause serious damage. They could take a beating better than any ships in the galaxy, although I was certainly going to put that to the test before the day was out.

"Tritium core is at 91 percent," Athena's voice rang in my ear.

Abby brought the *Renegade Star* in and released a volley of quad cannon missiles, striking the same spot I'd hit a second ago, and immediately retreated. She couldn't sit in the open for very long, not without drawing attention from the *Dawn*.

The blast opened the plating even further, creating more of a divide in the hull. I followed that with yet another blast, hoping to do as much damage as possible, no matter how small, in the few seconds we had.

The *Galactic Dawn*'s cannons turned and fired on my general position, but they couldn't seem to get a lock. Lucky for me, they still hadn't figured out how to target ancient Earth ships.

I dove forward, closer to the *Dawn*, nearly grazing its hull. An orange light flickered high above my position, which meant their shields had just activated. I was trapped inside, but that only meant I could do more damage.

I flew in close and hovered above the blind spot near the center of the ship, where the guns couldn't reach, then proceeded to fire several bursts of successive shots.

Brigham would have to make a choice, since he couldn't hit me from here. He'd have to either drop the shields and release his strike ships or sit here and take excessive damage.

Either way was fine with me.

I ordered my targeting system to aim for the engine section, then fired my beam cannon at the hull, slowly splitting it apart.

As I expected, the shields flickered off in short time. Brigham would send in his fighters to deal with me before I had a chance to fully disable his carrier, but that was ignorant thinking on his part.

There was more to this bird than a simple cannon.

With the hull open, I pulled in closer and imagined my ship dropping a mine—the same mines Athena had loaned me during our assault on Priscilla.

The bomb released from beneath me, shooting forward at the exact location I wanted—inside the broken hull.

I let myself grin. "Abby, I'm coming back! Get to *Titan!*"

"On our way," she returned.

I checked the radar to see the blue dot that represented the *Renegade Star* making its way to the gas giant. *Titan* was on the other side, still letting its core recharge.

While I observed the holo, a flood of red poured out from beneath my position. The strike ships, hundreds of them, were dispersing into open space. They would come for me first, but none of this was a surprise.

I brought my ship above the *Galactic Dawn,* speeding forward, between two raised cannons. Each of them took aim at me, firing torpedoes. I pulled up and then sideways, avoiding the projectiles. Since they couldn't lock on to me, the shots continued into the darkness, uninterrupted, while I followed the edge of the ship's hull, sticking close.

The other strike ships began moving after me, following my flight pattern. I stuck as close to the *Dawn* as possible.

Whatever shots they missed would hit the carrier, so I didn't let myself grow too far from it.

Multiple strike ships came up behind me, finally firing on my rear. Apparently, killing me was more important than the safety of their own starship. I'd take that as a compliment.

My vessel shook from the rear blast, but hardly enough to slow me down. It hadn't been a direct hit. Two other missiles flew past me and into the *Galactic Dawn's* hull. Lucky day, since that meant they still couldn't get a lock on me.

I cut thrusters and turned the ship so I was facing the attackers and returned fire. I sent a beam of blue energy straight directly into them, decimating six of the strike ships in a single blast. The other pursuing ships behind them dispersed like a flock of spooked birds.

I turned my ship around again, letting the others go. My enemy was bigger than all of them and far more dangerous. I brought my ship high above the *Galactic Dawn*, then leaned forward so that I could get the carrier in view.

I was staring at one of the most powerful vessels in the known galaxy, housing hundreds of smaller ships, and it was helmed by a seasoned general with decades of combat experience. Anyone watching from the outside might have thought this was a one-sided fight and that I was suicidal for even attempting it.

But he who controls the battlefield wins, and right now, I had the advantage.

I had a godsdamn moon.

"Athena, status check!" I snapped.

"Tritium core is at 95.6 percent," returned the Cognitive.

I grinned. "Good enough! Now bring that fat ass out here!"

"Understood."

The cannons on the *Dawn* fired on my position again, hitting my shields and jerking the entire ship. The blast sent me flying, but I managed to reorient myself in a few seconds.

My radar detected another set of missiles, headed straight for me. The old man must have figured out how to target me, finally.

It was good while it lasted.

I ordered my ship to push forward, away from the torpedoes. They followed me, gaining on my rear as I continued. I pulled around and aimed my cannon, shooting at the two bombs as they neared.

The blast struck the first missile, destroying it, while the second continued. I didn't have time to hit it, so I'd have to take the blast directly. I hoped my shields could handle it.

Right before the torpedo was about to reach my position, a beam of blue light struck its side and ignited the missile. I nearly fell back in my seat. "Holy—"

"Hey, Captain," said a voice over the com.

A ship swept across my screen, one that seemed to be identical to...

"Alphonse?" I asked, leaning forward. "Is that you?"

An image popped up on my screen, and I saw Alphonse from the waist up. He gave me a nod. "Sorry for the delay. It took some time to get these tattoos on me."

"I wasn't expecting you to make it out here, so I'll count this as a bonus," I said.

He smiled. "As will I, Captain."

"Stick close to me and try not to get shot, Al. We're heading back to Titan before things get out of hand."

"I'll follow your lead, sir," he said.

I brought my ship around to face the *Galactic Dawn*. "One last thing," I muttered, sending a mental command to the bomb I'd left behind.

Instantly, the hull of the *Galactic Dawn* exploded, ripping metal from metal, splitting a massive chunk of the ship away from the body. The lights of the *Dawn* flickered as pieces of the ship scattered into open space.

Brigham reacted by raising the orange shields on the carrier, but it was too late to fix what was already broken. He'd be working repairs on that carrier for months.

I turned my craft back toward the distant gas giant, enticing Brigham to follow.

I stared at my holo display and watched the *Galactic Dawn*, wondering if the old man was actually going to keep coming after me. He certainly hadn't shown any signs of stopping yet.

The massive red dot blinked, staying in the same position for longer than I felt comfortable with. I was about to turn around and fire on him again, when the carrier finally began to move.

I had to admit, even with a large chunk of its hull missing, the carrier ship was still intimidating. Hopefully, Brigham would feel the same when he saw my backup.

As we neared the gas giant, I spotted *Titan* hovering inside the planet's atmosphere. The *Renegade Star* was behind her, waiting for its chance to act.

The *Galactic Dawn* fired at *Titan*, using all of its remaining cannons. Hundreds of missiles left the carrier at once, filling the gap between the ships.

I approached the moon with enough firepower following me to glass a small planet. Was Brigham trying to destroy *Titan?* Either he was smart enough to know what it took to disable that ship or the opposite was true and he was trying to wipe it out completely.

Either way, I wagered it wouldn't matter. The old man had yet to witness *Titan's* true potential. He was about to have a rude awakening.

Alphonse and I brought our ships inside the safety zone of *Titan's* shield. Once there, I heard Athena's voice come over the com. "Activating shield."

I was barely inside when the blue wall appeared around *Titan* and multiple bombs collided with it, creating ripple after ripple as the shield absorbed the explosions. Less than a few seconds later, all of the missiles had landed and the shield was still holding.

I let myself breathe a short sigh of relief, then I remembered how close to death I'd just been, and I was suddenly tense again. "Alphonse, dock your ship and join the others. Abby and I will be there soon," I told him.

"Captain, I don't think I should abandon you," he responded.

"I'll be right behind you," I assured him. "You wanna be part of this crew? That means following orders."

"I understand," said Alphonse.

I watched him enter the orange and red clouds in the planet's atmosphere, disappearing as his ship drew closer to Titan.

At the same moment, countless strike ships filled my radar, leaving the *Galactic Dawn* and heading toward us. Titan was still inside the planet's upper atmosphere, half-hidden from the enemy's line-of-sight.

The swarm of ships came together in a crowded mass, flying through the void, toward Titan's position, exactly as I had hoped.

"Now's your chance, Athena!" I said, ordering my little ship to the rear of *Titan*, dipping far into the storm clouds. "Let those bastards have it!"

"Moving into position and deploying assault beam," informed the Cognitive. "Please stand by."

Titan moved through the clouds until the incoming fighters were in sight.

The glow of the shield around *Titan* dropped and several blue beams formed at various points around the ship, each of them several times larger than the one from my little vessel. They shot through the planet's atmosphere and out across the void, unleashing the wrath of a two-thousand-year-old civilization.

In a single breath, the blue beams tore through dozens of ships, breaking them to dust and scattering the rest. What few remained were either immobilized or forced into a spin.

I was taken aback by the sheer magnitude of the attack. I'd never seen anything so destructive.

The beam continued through the ships, toward the *Dawn*, plowing straight into its shields. The blast stopped after a moment, but Athena followed it with another, almost immediately.

Titan struck the *Dawn* a second time, not giving it a chance to retaliate. Athena followed that up with a wide spray of torpedoes, bombarding the *Galactic Dawn* with everything it had. The carrier withstood as much as it could before the shield collapsed, breaking apart like orange glass.

As the beam hit, it broke a huge chunk of the hull clean off, splintering the ship but not destroying it. The Union had built it well, with multiple reinforced layers of protection.

"Siggy, drop the lift," I sent. "I'm coming in."

"Of course, sir," answered the A.I.

I brought the little ship closer to the *Renegade Star*, right as the cargo bay opened. With little more than a thought, I ordered the vessel to deploy its landing gear and touch down on the floor, sealing its magnetic legs in place.

"Captain Hughes," said Athena. "Please be advised that multiple enemy vessels are approaching through the nearby tunnel."

"What are we looking at?" I asked, waiting briefly for the lift to close.

"Two additional carrier class starships are inbound. Each is equivalent to the estimated size of the *Galactic Dawn*," she answered.

I paused at the message, taken aback for a second at what I was hearing. "Did you say two more carriers?"

"Correct," she confirmed.

"Athena, you need to open a tunnel and move!" I snapped, leaping out of my chair. The ship door opened and I ran into the *Renegade Star*'s cargo bay, heading to the nearby stairs.

"What is your estimated time of arrival?" asked Athena.

"Just go!" I ordered. "Get out of their line-of-sight and head beneath the clouds again, then open that tunnel. We'll drop a few mines to slow them down, but we'll be right behind you!"

I made my way through the upper deck and into the corridor, racing toward the front of the ship. Abby's voice came over the com as I entered the lounge. "Jace? Where are you? What are we—"

I pulled open the door to the cockpit to see Abby and Freddie look at me. "Swap out," I said, motioning with my hand.

Abby stepped out of the seat, giving me room. "Siggy, stay close to *Titan* and prepare to deploy mines!"

"Understood," said Sigmond. "Welcome back, sir."

"Jace, what's going on?" asked Abigail.

"We're running," I said, not even bothering to strap myself in. "There's two more *Dawns* headed our way and I'm pretty sure we're boned if we stay."

"Even with *Titan*?" asked Freddie.

"I'm not chancing it," I said, glancing at him. "And get your ass in the back, Fred! The nun has a better eye for killin'. I need her on guns."

"R-right," he answered, getting to his feet.

Abby sat down in the co-pilot chair, bringing up weapon controls.

Athena's voice cut in. "Forming a new slip tunnel."

I was about to ask how long it would take, but I got the answer immediately. The rift began to form, surprising all of us as it split the atmosphere apart. Orange and yellow clouds swirled, turning darker as the green rift collided with them. "Holy shit," I said. "That didn't take long."

"It must be the new core," said Abigail.

"That is correct," answered Athena. "Entering slip-space in ten seconds."

"Is it safe to open a tunnel inside a planet's atmosphere?" asked Abby.

"We're about to find out," I muttered. "Athena, keep going. We'll be right behind you." I pulled the controls sticks and brought us out from behind *Titan*, moving out of the moon's flight path. "Siggy, how are those mines looking?"

"Ready for deployment, sir," said the A.I.

I looked at Abby. "Keep an eye on any strike ships they send at us. If they get close while we're deploying these things, we're dead."

"I'll handle it," she said with a short nod.

I took another breath, watching as *Titan* entered the tunnel. We only had a handful of seconds to get those mines in place before the enemy ships showed up.

So much for having a plan.

20

WE DEPLOYED about a dozen mines in record time, although that was only a third of our inventory. The *Galactic Dawn* was immobilized, but we were about to have more firepower at our backs than any of us could conceive.

Hell was breaking loose and quickly, and I felt the fire on my heels.

Titan had gone through the slip tunnel, expecting us to follow right away. The rift was still open too, and I knew better than to let it close. It would take far too long for us to get it back, and I honestly had no idea whether we could in this atmosphere. I just had to finish getting these mines—

A tunnel opened right behind The *Galactic Dawn*. Another carrier emerged, edging its way out of the rift at the same slow speed as its predecessor.

My eyes widened at the sight of another massive enemy ship. *Fuuuuuck.*

Before I could even turn to Abby and say the word I was thinking, a third ship flew in and arrived near the edge of the system, bringing a beeping red dot onto the holo display.

And there's number three.

"Uh oh," muttered Freddie.

"You said it." I touched the controls. "Siggy, let's follow the others. We need to go before the tunnel closes!"

"Understood," said the A.I.

Abby held the weapon controls in her hand. She had that look on her face, the kind that said she was ready to go down fighting if it came to it. Not that it would. I sure as hell wasn't ready to die, not here. Not in a place like this.

The slip engine hummed inside the belly of the *Renegade Star*, and a beam shot from beneath the cockpit, targeting the existing tear as it appeared before us. It only took a few seconds for the tunnel to widen back to its previous size, but it was all the time we needed.

Behind us, several dozen strike ships flew in our direction, headed straight for the minefield. I had played this game before, so I knew full well what Brigham was doing. He would sacrifice every last fighter if it meant stopping me here and now. He was a military man, which meant everything at his disposal was fodder, so long as it built towards his singular goal. All 10,000 of his soldiers would die if it meant he could have the prize... if it meant he could have Lex.

A few of the mines exploded as the fighters collided with them. The bombs didn't even have to move very far. It was like the ships were *trying* to hit them, like they knew they were on a suicide mission.

I began to move the *Star* into the rift, pressing the control sticks forward, easing us inside. "Steady now," I muttered.

"Hurry, Jace," said Abigail. "We don't have much time before they—"

A sudden explosion lit up the display as another ship collided with another bomb. Finally, there was a clean path through the field. That was my fault, I reckoned, since I had only managed to drop a short supply.

I just had to hurry before anyone else showed up.

"Incoming missile," said Sigmond.

"Screw it!" I snapped, pushing the control sticks forward as hard as I could, ignoring safety protocols for slipspace entry.

The radar showed the bomb headed towards us. "Turn the ship!" said Abigail.

I already knew where her head was at, so I didn't argue. I brought the *Star* around, cutting thrusters as we continued to move into the tunnel. When we were facing the oncoming missile, she took aim and fired a wide spray.

The bullets flew into the void, missing the torpedo. She tried again, but it was impossible enough to hit an actual ship under this kind of pressure, let alone a missile no bigger than a couple of meters.

Finally, as it drew closer, she landed a hit, tearing the bomb on its edge, sending it careening into the minefield. It drew close to one of the proximity mines before righting itself and resuming its run. The mine followed, closing in to the missile as both headed straight toward us.

Abby fired in a more focused spread, hitting the torpedo again, but this time with more accuracy. The missile was torn apart by the gunfire, exploding some distance from us as we began to ease into the slip tunnel, still facing the minefield.

The proximity mine continued in our direction, however, despite its target being annihilated. It seemed to want to keep going, and I didn't have the means to stop it.

The bomb flew right past us, into the slip tunnel, disappearing into the green lightning storm, missing the *Renegade Star* by what must have been ten meters.

A transmission broke across my com right as the rest of my ship entered the rift. A husky voice that I had grown far too familiar with spoke in a rather commanding tone, "Send everything you have! Follow that ship!"

The general must not have cared about privacy, since I was able to so easily pick it up on my com. Or maybe he simply didn't care. Maybe he wanted me to hear it.

Either way, we were gone, the tunnel closing behind us. Or was it ahead of us, since we were moving backwards? It didn't matter. The point was, we were finally moving.

"Adjusting movement to compensate for trajectory," said Sigmond.

"Does this mean we're in the clear?" asked Freddie.

"We're never in the clear," I said. "Haven't you learned that yet?"

I let Sigmond make the necessary corrections, since they'd require more attention to detail than any human brain could give. Constant micro-corrections every millisecond. Don't ask me.

"The *Dawn* might be immobilized, but those other two ships are going to follow us soon," said Abigail. She began to reflexively clench her hands. "We need to get aboard *Titan* as soon as we exit this tunnel."

I nodded. With a fully charged tritium core at her disposal, Athena no longer needed to stop to recharge. We could run forever, and probably faster than before. That was my hope anyway. "We can't contact *Titan* from here, so we'll just have to wait and see once we're out of this," I explained. "In the meantime, Freddie, let's you and me check on our other passenger. You know, make sure she's still alive."

"You mean Dressler?" he asked.

"Who else would I mean?" I pushed myself out of the chair. "Hopefully, she hasn't starved to death."

Abigail touched my wrist as I stepped between our seats. "Are you actually going to let her go?"

I shrugged. "She hasn't done us any wrong. The way I see it, she deserves what was promised. If we make it clear of here, I'll give her the shuttle and she can hightail it to whatever she thinks freedom is."

FREDDIE and I left the bridge and made our way straight to the doc's room. "Open it," I said, standing before the door.

"Yes, sir," said Sigmond, and the door slid open.

Dressler was sitting on the bed with her hands across her chest, like she hadn't expected to see us. She jumped to her feet. "Y-you're back!"

"Sorry to keep you waiting, Doc," I said, stepping in.

"What's going on out there? I've been trying to converse with Sigmond for the last thirty minutes, but he isn't the most talkative A.I.," said Dressler.

"That's because he's been busy focusing on the fight. I'm surprised he had enough time to talk to you at all," I said.

"It would have been poor manners to ignore our guest," said Sigmond. "I do apologize for my lack of attention, Doctor."

Dressler seemed to break a smile before putting it away and narrowing her eyes at me. "Well, then, would you care to explain the situation, now that you're here?"

"We took out a few dozen strike ships, killed the engines on the *Galactic Dawn* so they couldn't follow us, and jumped into a new slip tunnel before the rest of the fleet could catch us. We're on our way to meet with *Titan* right now," I said, fanning my hand at her. "Simple day, simple way."

She blinked. "You took on General Brigham's carrier ship? Sigmond mentioned that he had arrived, but what you're saying sounds…unlikely."

"Believe what you want," I said with a shrug. "Either way, it happened, and now he's sitting on his own tail, trying to figure out how to catch us. Without a working slip engine, he's going to have a rough go of it."

Dressler's mouth dropped. "Y-you're being serious? If you attacked General Brigham, the entire Union fleet is going to come after you!" She darted her eyes to Fred. "Is he telling the truth?"

Freddie nodded. "The Captain used a strike ship from *Titan* and penetrated Brigham's defenses. He nearly took the entire carrier out on his own."

The doctor cocked her brow at me, and for a quick second, it looked like a sign of respect. "I can't believe it."

"Affirmative," said Sigmond. "If you are interested, I can replay the video feed from the encounter."

The doctor seemed to consider the idea, but then dismissed it. "No, it doesn't matter. We had a deal for that shuttle, didn't we?"

I smirked. "Figures you'd still want to leave, lady. But sure, you can have the shuttle," I said, then nodded in the direction of the window. Green swirls moved past us, along the slip tunnel walls. "Once we're out of slipspace."

"How long?"

"Beats the hell outta me," I said. "What do you say, Siggy?"

"Based on the tunnel's current approximate length, I estimate another three hours of flight time before we arrive," explained the A.I.

"See?" I said to the doctor. "Not that long and you'll be a free citizen. You can fly back to the Union and tell them all about your evil captors."

She nodded slowly, like she was mulling over what I'd said.

I stared at her for a moment, waiting to see if she had any other questions. She didn't, so I took a step back. I was about to say goodbye, when Sigmond's voice broke the silence. "Sir, if I might have your attention." His voice was coming through my com, I quickly realized.

I touched my ear and turned away from the others. "What is it?"

"I'm detecting an energy spike in the tunnel ahead of us," said Sigmond.

"I thought we couldn't see any other ships," I responded.

"That is still correct. However, while we are unable to detect movement, energy distortions are still occurring—"

"English, Siggy," I interrupted.

"Yes, sir. In short, when an object interacts with the slip tunnel's boundaries directly, it creates a vibration, which is detectable by our long-range sensors."

"What's wrong, Captain?" asked Dressler, who was

standing a few steps behind me. I'd almost forgotten she and Freddie were there.

I held up my index finger. "Hold on, Doc," I said, then touched my ear. "Siggy, what's the most likely cause?"

"Based on the size of the vibrations along the tunnel walls, I would estimate that a reaction has occurred," said Sigmond. "I believe the source to be the proximity mine that we witnessed entering the tunnel."

"How bad is it?" I asked.

Both Dressler and Freddie drew closer at the sound of the question. I could almost feel their tension clouding around me. It made me feel claustrophobic, so I threw my hand out to tell them to give me some space.

"The actual damage is unknown," explained Sigmond. "However, given the magnitude of the explosive, it is possible that the tunnel has taken on severe damage."

My eyes went wide with the possible repercussions of what I had just heard. "Crap," I muttered, turning to finally address the other two in the room.

"Don't tell me," said Freddie, swallowing the lump in his throat. "We're not in the clear, are we?"

"Not even close," I answered.

THE SLIPSPACE RUPTURE was worse than I thought.

The shockwave caused by the proximity mine explosion

hit us a few minutes after Siggy told us about it, nearly knocking us all on our asses.

I held myself up on the wall, while Dressler collapsed back into the bed. Freddie, meanwhile, stayed on his feet, using the bedpost as leverage.

"Abigail to Jace!" screamed a voice in my ear. "I need you on the bridge!"

I tried to take a step towards the door but nearly dropped. "Not happening! I can't move!"

"Siggy says the mine blew up," said Abby.

"Probably broke the tunnel," I shouted. "Try to compensate!"

"Compensation is futile," said Sigmond. "Please brace for impact."

Dressler, Freddie, and I exchanged a mutual horrified look of uncertainty. "You've got to be kidding me," I said in a tone that suggested we were royally screwed.

Before either could answer, the *Star* shook even harder, like it had been saving the bulk of its fury up, only to let it all come crashing out. Freddie finally hit the floor, slamming his face into the carpet, while Dressler tossed in the bed. I stayed on my knees, using the wall and floor as leverage. It wasn't enough, however, and I finally went flying.

I slammed into Freddie, hitting him in the nose with my knee (poor guy). He screamed, and I was pretty sure I saw blood, but I couldn't worry about that right now. There was a decent chance we were all about to die.

"Entering slipspace rupture," said Sigmond, his voice as

steady as ever. Sometimes I really hated how calm he could be.

The ship continued to shake, throwing both Freddie and me around the floor and into the wall, back where I started.

For a second, I thought the ship might tear itself apart from the inside, but the turbulence stopped before I could express it, and we came flying out of the tunnel in a few short seconds.

With a steady floor beneath me, I eased myself back on my feet, although I still felt like I was half-drunk and disoriented.

I shook it off and, without another word, staggered my way out of the room and toward the bridge. It was time to figure out exactly where the hell we were.

For better or worse.

I ENTERED the cockpit to find Abigail looking like she was desperate for a skull to bash. I could sense the frustration, thick as smog. "What's our status?" I asked.

"What do you think?" she balked, pulling up a holo of the star system we'd just entered. "We're stranded in the middle of nowhere."

"Nowhere?" I asked, looking over the seven planets and three asteroid belts. "Siggy, where are we?"

"Unknown, sir," said the A.I.

"What do you mean, 'unknown'?" I asked.

"Star layout matches no previous model, nor can I extrapolate our position."

I heard movement behind me, but I didn't have to look to know who it was. "How bad is it?" asked Freddie, standing beside the door.

Dressler was with him, but she didn't say anything.

"Bad," I muttered. "We're in unknown space, and since we entered that tunnel without knowing the destination, it's hard to tell exactly where we are. We could have been dropped off literally anywhere, in any direction."

"Can't Sigmond read the star chart?" asked Fred.

"That only works if the stars match what we have in the database," I said.

"Correct," said Sigmond. "The layout before us is foreign. No records of it exist, which implies this is a region outside of known space."

"Outside?" asked Dressler, who had finally chosen to speak up. "Are you saying we've moved beyond civilized Union space?"

"More than that," I said, nodding at the nearby yellow star at the center of this system. "If there's no record, that means no one has ever come this far. We're not in the Deadlands, the Sarkonian Empire, or Union space."

"But we were only in the tunnel for fifteen minutes," said Freddie.

"Tunnels are funny like that," I said. "Real space distance doesn't matter. Only the slipspace inside matters, and no two tunnels are the same. That one was brand new, thanks to *Titan*, so there's no knowing how far it actually went. Who the hell knows where we ended up?"

"That's not very encouraging," muttered Fred.

"Can we get back inside the tunnel?" asked Abigail.

"I'm afraid that won't be possible," said Sigmond. "According to sensors, there is no longer a tunnel to return back to."

We all looked at each other. "Siggy, what do you mean there's no longer a tunnel?" I asked.

"I do not know," admitted the A.I. "Sensors are no longer showing an entry point for the slip tunnel, and I lack the necessary data to make a determined conclusion."

Abigail leaned forward and slammed her palm on the dash. "Theorize!"

"It is possible that the tunnel resealed itself moments after the mine detonated," said Siggy. "Slipspace tunnels have broken before, but they do not always remain so. Additionally, even if I could detect the tunnel entrance, I'm sorry to say that we would not be able to use it. The damage from the turbulence has put too much strain on our engines. Not only is the slipspace engine currently disabled, but so are long-range thrusters."

"Are you saying we couldn't open a tunnel even if we had one in front of us?" asked Abigail.

"Indeed, Ms. Pryar," confirmed the A.I.

"Great," said Abigail, tossing up her hands. "Out of one mess and into another."

I had to admit, Abigail was right. We'd escaped Brigham's attack by the skin of our teeth, only to wind up in the middle of nowhere, surrounded by unknown stars. Without a reference point, there was no way we'd be able to chart the right course, even if we could get our engines back online.

"Should we wait here for *Titan*?" asked Freddie. He was staring at me with puppy dog eyes, desperate for a solution.

I waited a second before answering, weighing what few options I had. "Siggy, how are your sensors?" I finally asked.

"Working," he said.

"Scan the system and look for anything that might be useful," I said.

"Already processing, sir," said Sigmond.

"Any signs of other slip tunnels?" I asked.

"None within three star systems," answered Sigmond. "I apologize, sir."

Abigail and I looked at each other. "What now?" she asked, all the frustration in her voice finally dissipated. If I didn't know any better, I might have called it defeat.

"We have no choice," I said, shaking my head. "We'll have to wait here for *Titan* to come find us."

"You think Athena even knows where to look?" asked Freddie.

"We'd better hope she does," I muttered, glancing at the holo display of the star system. "As bad as it was back there with Brigham, the last thing you want is to be stranded and lost."

"You talk about it like you've done it before," said Dressler.

I nodded. "Lady, you don't know the half of it."

EPILOGUE

I WAITED for the scans to come in, while Freddie, Dressler, and Abigail went to check on the slipspace engine. Dressler was a trained scientist, so I figured if anyone on this ship could get things moving again, it was her. I just didn't trust her enough to let her go alone.

"Sir, I believe I've found something," said Sigmond.

"Put it on the holo," I muttered.

A readout appeared with a full list of planets and moons in the system. Most were lifeless or too inhospitable to bother with, except for a class-5 world, resting in the comfort zone around the star.

Class-5 meant that it had a breathable atmosphere, probably contained carbon-based life, and had a fair chance of having edible food, but it wasn't ideal.

"What am I looking at, Siggy? You know a class-5 isn't worth landing on," I said, leaning back in my seat. "We'd be fools to try."

"Of course, sir," said the A.I. "However, the planet itself is not what interests me."

I cocked my brow. "Then why are you showing it to me?"

"I am detecting a faint transmission, sir," said Sigmond.

"A transmission?" I asked, perking up. "Is it Union?"

"I don't believe so," said Siggy. "The signature is unknown, and it is too distorted to fully uncover, but I believe it is a request for help."

"Where's it coming from?" I asked.

The holo zoomed in on the planet, showing a landscape covered in ice, nearly barren. "Here," said Sigmond, right as a red dot appeared on the globe. "Somewhere beneath the ice. Please, sir, one moment. I am attempting to recover the message."

I stared at the holo, narrowing my eyes. How could there be a message in a place like this, so far from an existing slip tunnel?

"The message seems to be in another language," continued Sigmond.

"Which language?" I asked.

The message erupted over the speaker, playing in a broken, static-filled voice. It was a woman, by the sound of it.

"Sir, I believe this is a dialect of a language in my database," said Sigmond. "The same language that *Titan*'s original colonists used, although this one is very far removed, with many changes."

"*Titan?*" I asked, taken aback by what I was hearing. How could this person be using the same language as the people on *Titan* from over two thousand years ago? Could some of the colonists have come here, while the other survivors went off in other directions? That was possible, I supposed, but it didn't explain the lack of slip tunnels nearby or why exactly anyone would land on a planet like this one. There were countless habitable worlds out there that were better than this.

Unless they crashed, of course. "Can you translate it?" I asked.

"I believe so, sir," said Sigmond.

I took the controls and began flying us closer to the planet, mostly trying to stay busy while I waited for Sigmond to do his job. It only took a few moments to get the *Renegade Star* in orbit, and then I waited for more answers.

After several minutes, Sigmond finally spoke again. "Playing translation. Stand by."

The female voice came back over the com, but this time, she spoke in a language I understood. "Attention, this world is the property of Earth. All Transient vessels should avoid orbit or risk defense network capabilities, per the established colonization agreement."

"Earth?" I asked, sitting up. Of all the things I had

expected to hear, that sure as hell wasn't one of them. "Siggy, are you positive that's what she said?"

"I am certain of nothing, sir. This is a completely foreign language. It could be a mistranslation, depending on a number of variables. The word 'Earth' could have multiple meanings for this speaker."

I cracked a smile. "Fair enough," I said, then touched the floating globe on my dash and zoomed in on the spot where the transmission was coming from. "You think you could land us near this, Siggy?"

"There is a small field nearby," said the A.I.

"Good," I said, reaching up for my harness. I pulled it over my chest and locked it in place. "You know I've never been able to walk away from a threatening, ominous voice, Siggy."

"That much I know," agreed the A.I.

"Do you think whoever sent that is still alive?" I asked.

"I am detecting life signs across the continent, many of which are near that location," informed Sigmond. "Interference from the local snowstorms makes specific analysis impossible, however."

I grinned, staring at the holo display. "Good enough for me," I said, pressing the control stick forward. "What do you say, Siggy? Let's see if we can find ourselves some neighbors."

Want to continue the story? Renegade Lost is out right now, exclusively on Amazon.

Read on for a special note from the author.

AUTHOR NOTES

Boy, time sure does get away from you sometimes, doesn't it? The last six weeks have been filled with chaos. After a writer's conference in Vegas, a serious bout with the flu, and another book release, I still managed to get *Renegade Moon* written and published. It was definitely the toughest book to release on time, but somehow, it all came together.

Jace and Abigail managed to find the power source they needed to keep *Titan* floating, which brought them even closer to General Brigham than ever before. They pulled through, however, and managed to best the Union again. Not bad for a Renegade and a nun.

The team also learned about the history of Earth, at least in part. This was something I've wanted to share from the very beginning, but I had to wait for the story to get there. I know many readers were wondering how the galaxy (and humanity) came to be this way, so I'm happy to finally share that aspect of the lore.

Finally, there's something else I wanted to touch on in this book that many of you have been asking for, which is Jace's history. To date, I've avoided talking too much about Jace's past, because I was more interested in showing him in real time and letting his decisions show his nature. Now that we've had a few books to see what kind of man he is, it seemed like the right time to get in there and find out what started Jace on this whole Renegade journey. There's still a lot more to learn about him, of course, and we'll visit those memories in due time, but I wanted to share a glimpse of that history with you, because I think it's important if we want to understand him.

All of that being said, I hope you enjoyed this latest entry in the *Renegade Star series*. The next entry will be out in early January, so you won't have to wait very long. Get ready for more secrets and startling revelations as we reach *Renegade Lost,* part four in this epic space opera saga.

I'll see you soon, Renegades,

J.N. Chaney

PS. Amazon won't tell you when the next Renegade book will come out, but there are several ways you can stay informed.

1) **Fly on over to the Facebook group, JN**

Chaney's Renegade Readers, and say hello. It's a great place to hang with other sarcastic sci-fi readers who don't mind a good laugh.

2) **Follow me directly on Amazon**. To do this, head to the **store page** for this book (or my Amazon author profile) and click the Follow button beneath my picture. That will prompt Amazon to notify you when I release a new book. You'll just need to check your emails.

3) **You can join my mailing list by clicking here**. This will allow me to stay in touch with you directly, and you'll also receive a free copy of The Amber Project.

Doing one of these or **all three** (for best results) will ensure you know every time a new entry in *the Renegade Star series* is published. Please take a moment to do one of these so you'll be able to join Jace, Abigail, and Lex on their next galaxy-spanning adventure.

PREVIEW: THE AMBER PROJECT

Documents of Historical, Scientific, and Cultural Significance
Play Audio Transmission File 021
Recorded April 19, 2157

CARTWRIGHT: *This is Lieutenant Colonel Felix Cartwright. It's been a week since my last transmission and two months since the day we found the city...the day the world fell apart. If anyone can hear this, please respond.*

If you're out there, no doubt you know about the gas. You might think you're all that's left. But if you're receiving this, let me assure you, you are not alone. There are people here. Hundreds, in fact, and for now, we're safe. If you can make it here, you will be, too.

The city's a few miles underground, not far from El Rico Air Force Base. That's where my people came from. As always, the coordi-

nates are attached. If anyone gets this, please respond. Let us know you're there…that you're still alive.

End Audio File

April 14, 2339

Maternity District

MILES BELOW THE SURFACE OF THE EARTH, deep within the walls of the last human city, a little boy named Terry played quietly with his sister in a small two-bedroom apartment.

Today was his very first birthday. He was turning seven.

"What's a birthday?" his sister Janice asked, tugging at his shirt. She was only four years old and had recently taken to following her big brother everywhere he went. "What does it mean?"

Terry smiled, eager to explain. "Mom says when you turn seven, you get a birthday. It means you grow up and get to start school. It's a pretty big deal."

"When will I get a birthday?"

"You're only four, so you have to wait."

"I wish I was seven," she said softly, her thin black hair hanging over her eyes. "I want to go with you."

He got to his feet and began putting the toy blocks away. They had built a castle together on the floor, but

Mother would yell if they left a mess. "I'll tell you all about it when I get home. I promise, okay?"

"Okay!" she said cheerily and proceeded to help.

Right at that moment, the speaker next to the door let out a soft chime, followed by their mother's voice. "Downstairs, children," she said. "Hurry up now."

Terry took his sister's hand. "Come on, Jan," he said.

She frowned, squeezing his fingers. "Okay."

They arrived downstairs, their mother nowhere to be found.

"She's in the kitchen," Janice said, pointing at the farthest wall. "See the light-box?"

Terry looked at the locator board, although his sister's name for it worked just as well. It was a map of the entire apartment, with small lights going on and off in different colors, depending on which person was in which room. *There's us,* he thought, *green for me and blue for Janice, and there's Mother in red.* Terry never understood why they needed something like that because of how small the apartment was, but every family got one, or so Mother had said.

As he entered the kitchen, his mother stood at the far counter sorting through some data on her pad. "What's that?" he asked.

"Something for work," she said. She tapped the front of the pad and placed it in her bag. "Come on, Terrance, we've got to get you ready and out the door. Today's your first day, after all, and we have to make a good impression."

"When will he be back?" asked Janice.

"Hurry up. Let's go, Terrance," she said, ignoring the question. She grabbed his hand and pulled him along. "We have about twenty minutes to get all the way to the education district. Hardly enough time at all." Her voice was sour. He had noticed it more and more lately, as the weeks went on, ever since a few months ago when that man from the school came to visit. His name was Mr. Huxley, one of the few men who Terry ever had the chance to talk to, and from the way Mother acted—she was so agitated—he must have been important.

"Terrance." His mother's voice pulled him back. "Stop moping and let's go."

Janice ran and hugged him, wrapping her little arms as far around him as she could. "Love you," she said.

"Love you too."

"Bye," she said shyly.

He kissed her forehead and walked to the door, where his mother stood talking with the babysitter, Ms. Cartwright. "I'll only be a few hours," Mother said. "If it takes any longer, I'll message you."

"Don't worry about a thing, Mara," Ms. Cartwright assured her. "You take all the time you need."

Mother turned to him. "There you are," she said, taking his hand. "Come on, or we'll be late."

As they left the apartment, Mother's hand tugging him along, Terry tried to imagine what might happen at school today. Would it be like his home lessons? Would he be behind the other children, or was everything new? He enjoyed learning, but there was still a chance the school might be too hard for him. What would he do? Mother had taught him some things, like algebra and English, but who knew how far along the other kids were by now?

Terry walked quietly down the overcrowded corridors with an empty, troubled head. He hated this part of the district. So many people on the move, brushing against him, like clothes in an overstuffed closet.

He raised his head, nearly running into a woman and her baby. She had wrapped the child in a green and brown cloth, securing it against her chest. "Excuse me," he said, but the lady ignored him.

His mother paused and looked around. "Terrance, what are you doing? I'm over here," she said, spotting him.

"Sorry."

They waited together for the train, which was running a few minutes behind today.

"I wish they'd hurry up," said a nearby lady. She was young, about fifteen years old. "Do you think it's because of the outbreak?"

"Of course," said a much older woman. "Some of the trains are busy carrying contractors to the slums to patch the walls. It slows the others down because now they have to make more stops."

"I heard fourteen workers died. Is it true?"

"You know how the gas is," she said. "It's very quick. Thank God for the quarantine barriers."

Suddenly, there was a loud smashing sound, followed by

three long beeps. It echoed through the platform for a moment, vibrating along the walls until it was gone. Terry flinched, squeezing his mother's hand.

"Ouch," she said. "Terrance, relax."

"But the sound," he said.

"It's the contractors over there." She pointed to the other side of the tracks, far away from them. It took a moment for Terry to spot them, but once he did, it felt obvious. Four of them stood together. Their clothes were orange, with no clear distinction between their shirts and their pants, and on each of their heads was a solid red plastic hat. Three of them were holding tools, huddled against a distant wall. They were reaching inside of it, exchanging tools every once in a while, until eventually the fourth one called them to back away. As they made some room, steam rose from the hole, with a puddle of dark liquid forming at the base. The fourth contractor handled a machine several feet from the others, which had three legs and rose to his chest. He waved the other four to stand near him and pressed the pad on the machine. Together, the contractors watched as the device flashed a series of small bright lights. It only lasted a few seconds. Once it was over, they gathered close to the wall again and resumed their work.

"What are they doing?" Terry asked.

His mother looked down at him. "What? Oh, they're fixing the wall, that's all."

"Why?" he asked.

"Probably because there was a shift last night. Remember when the ground shook?"

Yeah, I remember, he thought. *It woke me up.* "So they're fixing it?"

"Yes, right." She sighed and looked around. "Where is that damned train?"

Terry tugged on her hand. "That lady over there said it's late because of the gas."

His mother looked at him. "What did you say?"

"The lady...the one right there." He pointed to the younger girl a few feet away. "She said the gas came, so that's why the trains are slow. It's because of the slums." He paused a minute. "No, wait. It's because they're *going* to the slums."

His mother stared at the girl, turning back to the tracks and saying nothing.

"Mother?" he said.

"Be quiet for a moment, Terrance."

Terry wanted to ask her what was wrong, or if he had done anything to upset her, but he knew when to stay silent. So he left it alone like she wanted. Just like a good little boy.

The sound of the arriving train filled the platform with such horrific noise that it made Terry's ears hurt. The train, still vibrating as he stepped onboard, felt like it was alive.

After a short moment, the doors closed. The train was moving.

Terry didn't know if the shaking was normal or not. Mother had taken him up to the medical wards on this train once when he was younger, but never again after that. He didn't remember much about it, except that he liked it. The medical wards were pretty close to where he lived, a few stops before the labs, and several stops before the education district. After that, the train ran through Pepper Plaza, then the food farms and Housing Districts 04 through 07 and finally the outer ring factories and the farms. As Terry stared at the route map on the side of the train wall, memorizing what he could of it, he tried to imagine all the places he could go and the things he might see. What kind of shops did the shopping plaza have, for example, and what was it like to work on the farms? Maybe one day he could go and find out for himself—ride the train all day to see everything there was to see. Boy, wouldn't that be something?

"Departure call: 22-10, education district," erupted the com in its monotone voice. It took only a moment before the train began to slow.

"That's us. Come on," said Mother. She grasped his hand, pulling him through the doors before they were fully opened.

Almost to the school, Terry thought. He felt warm suddenly. Was he getting nervous? And why now? He'd known about this forever, and it was only hitting him *now?*

He kept taking shorter breaths. He wanted to pull away and return home, but Mother's grasp was tight and firm, and the closer they got to the only major building in the area, the tighter and firmer it became.

Now that he was there, now that the time had finally come, a dozen questions ran through Terry's mind. Would the other kids like him? What if he wasn't as smart as everyone else? Would they make fun of him? He had no idea what to expect.

Terry swallowed, the lump in his throat nearly choking him.

An older man stood at the gate of the school's entrance. He dressed in an outfit that didn't resemble any of the clothes in Terry's district or even on the trains. A gray uniform—the color of the pavement, the walls, and the streets—matched his silver hair to the point where it was difficult to tell where one ended and the other began. "Ah," he said. "Mara, I see you've brought another student. I was wondering when we'd meet the next one. Glad to see you're still producing. It's been, what? Five or six years? Something like that, I think."

"Yes, thank you, this is Terrance," said Mother quickly. "I was told there would be an escort." She paused, glancing over the man and through the windows. "Where's Bishop? He assured me he'd be here for this."

"The *colonel*," he corrected, "is in his office, and the boy is to be taken directly to him as soon as I have registered his arrival."

She let out a frustrated sigh. "He was supposed to meet me at the gate for this himself. I wanted to talk to him about a few things."

"What's wrong?" Terry asked.

She looked down at him. "Oh, it's nothing, don't worry. You have to go inside now, that's all."

"You're not coming in?"

"I'm afraid not," said the man. "She's not permitted."

"It's all right," Mother said, cupping her hand over his cheek. "They'll take care of you in there."

But it's just school, Terry thought. "I'll see you tonight, though, right?"

She bent down and embraced him tightly, more than she had in a long time. He couldn't help but relax. "I'm sorry, Terrance. Please be careful up there. I know you don't understand it now, but you will eventually. Everything will be fine." She rose, releasing his hand for the first time since they left the train. "So that's it?" Mother said to the man.

"Yes, ma'am."

"Good." She turned and walked away, pausing a moment as she reached the corner and continued until she was out of sight.

The man pulled out a board with a piece of paper on it. "When you go through here, head straight to the back of the hall. A guard there will take you to see Colonel Bishop. Just do what they say and answer everything with either 'Yes, sir' or 'No, sir,' and you'll be fine. Understand?"

Terry didn't understand, but he nodded anyway.

The man pushed open the door with his arm and leg, holding it there and waiting. "Right through here you go," he said.

Terry entered, reluctantly, and the door closed quickly behind him.

The building, full of the same metal and shades of brown and gray that held together the rest of the city, rose higher than any other building Terry had ever been in. Around the room, perched walkways circled the walls, cluttered with doors and hallways that branched off into unknown regions. Along the walkways, dozens of people walked back and forth as busily as they had in the train station. More importantly, Terry quickly realized, most of them were men.

For so long, the only men he had seen were the maintenance workers who came and went or the occasional teacher who visited the children when they were nearing their birthdays. It was so rare to see any men at all, especially in such great numbers. *Maybe they're all teachers*, he thought. They weren't dressed like the workers: white coats and some with brown jackets—thick jackets with laced boots and bodies as stiff as the walls. Maybe that was what teachers wore. How could he know? He had never met one besides Mr. Huxley, and that was months ago.

"Well, don't just stand there gawking," said a voice from the other end of the room. It was another man, dressed the same as the others. "Go on in through here." He pointed to another door, smaller than the one Terry had entered from. "Everyone today gets to meet the colonel. Go on now. Hurry up. You don't want to keep him waiting."

Terry did as the man said and stepped through the

doorway, his footsteps clanking against the hard metal floor, echoing through what sounded like the entire building.

"Well, come in, why don't you?" came a voice from inside.

Terry stepped cautiously into the room, which was much nicer than the entranceway. It was clean, at least compared to some of the other places Terry had been, including his own home. The walls held several shelves, none of which lacked for any company of things. Various ornaments caught Terry's eye, like the little see-through globe on the shelf nearest to the door, which held a picture of a woman's face inside, although some of it was faded and hard to make out. There was also a crack in it. What purpose could such a thing have? Terry couldn't begin to guess. Next to it lay a frame with a small, round piece of metal inside of it. An inscription below the glass read, "U.S. Silver Dollar, circa 2064." Terry could easily read the words, but he didn't understand them. What was this thing? And why was it so important that it needed to be placed on a shelf for everyone to look at?

"I said come in," said Bishop abruptly. He sat at the far end of the room behind a large brown desk. Terry had forgotten he was even there. "I didn't mean for you to stop at the door. Come over here."

Terry hurried closer, stopping a few feet in front of the desk.

"I'm Colonel Bishop. You must be Terrance," said the man. "I've been wondering when you were going to show up." He wore a pair of thin glasses and had one of the larger pads in his hand. "Already seven. Imagine that."

"Yes, sir," Terry said, remembering the doorman's words.

The colonel was a stout man, a little wider than the others. He was older too, Terry guessed. He may have been tall, but it was difficult to tell without seeing his whole body. "I expect you're hoping to begin your classes now," said Bishop.

"Yes, sir," he said.

"You say that, but you don't really know what you're saying yes to, do you?"

The question seemed more like a statement, so Terry didn't answer. He only stood there. Who was this man? Was this how school was supposed to be?

"Terrance, let me ask you something," said the colonel, taking a moment. "Did your mother tell you anything about this program you're going into?"

Terry thought about the question for a moment. "Um, she said you come to school on your birthday," he said. "And that it's just like it is at home, except there's more kids like me."

Colonel Bishop blinked. "That's right, I suppose. What else did she say?"

"That when it was over, I get to go back home," he said.

"And when did she say that was?"

Terry didn't answer.

Colonel Bishop cocked an eyebrow. "Well? Didn't she say?"

"No, sir," muttered Terry.

The man behind the desk started chuckling. "So you don't know how long you're here for?"

"No, sir."

Colonel Bishop set the pad in his hand down. "Son, you're here for the next ten years."

A sudden rush swelled up in Terry's chest and face. What was Bishop talking about? Of course Terry was going home. He couldn't stay here. "But I promised my sister I'd be home today," he said. "I have to go back."

"Too bad," said the colonel. "Your mother really did you a disservice by not telling you. But don't worry. We just have to get you started." He tapped the pad on his desk, and the door opened. A cluster of footsteps filled the hall before two large men appeared, each wearing the same brown coats as the rest. "Well, that was fast," he said.

One of the men saluted. "Yes, sir. No crying with the last one. Took her right to her room without incident."

Terry wanted to ask who *the last one* was, and why it should be a good thing that she didn't cry. Did other kids cry when they came to this school? What kind of place *was* this?

"Well, hopefully, Terrence here will do the same," said Bishop. He looked at Terry. "Right? You're not going to give us any trouble, are you?"

Terry didn't know what to do or what to say. All he

could think about was getting far away from here. He didn't want to go with the men. He didn't want to behave. All he wanted to do was go home.

But he couldn't, not anymore. He was here in this place with nowhere to go. No way out. He wanted to scream, to yell at the man behind the desk and his two friends, and tell them about how stupid it was for them to do what they were doing.

He opened his mouth to explain, to scream as loud as he could that he wouldn't go. But in that moment, the memory of the doorman came back to him, and instead of yelling, he repeated the words he'd been told before. "No, sir," he said softly.

Bishop smiled, nodding at the two men in the doorway. "Exactly what I like to hear."

Get the Amber Project now, exclusively on Amazon

GET A FREE BOOK

Chaney posts updates, official art, previews, and other awesome stuff on his website. You can also follow him on Instagram, Facebook, and Twitter.

Search for **JN Chaney's Renegade Readers** on Facebook to join the group where readers can come together and share their lives and interests, especially regarding Chaney's books.

For updates about new releases, as well as exclusive promotions, sign up for the VIP mailing list. Head there now to receive a free copy of *The Other Side of Nowhere*.

https://www.subscribepage.com/organic

Enjoying the series? Help others discover the Variant Saga by leaving a review on Amazon.

BOOKS BY J.N. CHANEY

ABOUT THE AUTHOR

J. N. Chaney has a Master's of Fine Arts in creative writing and fancies himself quite the Super Mario Bros. fan. When he isn't writing or gaming, you can find him online at **www.jnchaney.com**.

He migrates often but was last seen in Avon Park, Florida. Any sightings should be reported, as they are rare.

Renegade Moon is his eighth novel.

Made in the
USA
Middletown, DE